800208292

THE ITALIAN'S UNEXPECTED HEIR

THE ITALIAN'S UNEXPECTED HEIR

JENNIFER FAYE

MILLS & BOON

First published in Great Britain 2020
by Mills & Boon, an imprint of HarperCollins*Publishers*
1 London Bridge Street, London, SE1 9GF

Large Print edition 2021

ISBN: 978-0-263-28980-0

MIX
Paper from
responsible sources
FSC C007454

This book is produced from independently certified FSC™ paper to ensure responsible forest management. For more information visit www.harpercollins.co.uk/green.

Printed and bound in Great Britain
by CPI Group (UK) Ltd, Croydon, CR0 4YY

PROLOGUE

It took almost losing everything...
to make peace with a troubling past
and embrace a loving future

Paris, France, July

"CONGRATULATIONS! I KNEW you could do it."

Enzo Bartolini turned to the beautiful woman standing next to him. The excitement in her voice and the sparkle in her eyes let him know she was more excited about this evening's crowning achievement than he was. And that was the exact opposite of how things should be.

He was supposed to be the excited one—the one who felt as though he was on top of the world. This win was something he'd dreamed of for years. And now that it was here—now that he was holding the plaque with his name on it—the victory felt hollow.

The exhilaration he'd envisioned for this auspicious moment eluded him. The feeling of accomplishment—of finally being worthy of his father's praise—was not to be. Shadows of the past smothered the brightness of the moment.

Still, Enzo forced a bittersweet smile to his face. In truth, he hadn't truly won anything—at least nothing he felt worthy of claiming.

He'd encouraged his father for years to start entering his wine in competitions. Enzo knew the worldwide recognition would increase the demand for the wine and in turn raise its value. But his father had been stubborn, as usual. He'd said it was enough for him that he got to work the land each day and make a sizable profit. He didn't need awards or recognition, too.

However, Enzo needed it. He needed something to fill the huge gaping emptiness inside his chest. It had once been filled by the constant love of his parents, but they had been ripped from his life. In the time it took his parents to drive to the city for what? Groceries? Supplies for the vineyard? Whatever it was they'd set out to do that day, it had led to a horrific accident and forever changed the lives of their son and two daughters.

When Enzo had insisted on seeing the accident photos, his stomach retched. Perhaps he shouldn't have insisted. Perhaps he should have just taken the word of the police. But he'd been in shock, unable to process a life without his very dynamic parents in it. He'd demanded proof.

And then he'd been shown the photos. He'd only needed to see the one—the photo of a tangled-up piece of metal. It hadn't even resembled a car any longer. There was no chance his parents could have survived. None at all. Thinking there couldn't be anything else to compare to that devastation, he'd been wrong.

Enzo pushed aside those troubling thoughts. Tonight was all about the win. At last, there was once again something good in his life. So then why didn't it feel good? Why wasn't he on top of the world?

He reached to undo his black bow tie as well as loosen the top button of his white dress shirt, when Sylvie said, "Don't. Not yet. I need a picture of you first."

His hand hesitated in midair before he lowered it to his side.

Over the past several months, Sylvie DeLuca

had become a good friend. She had the brightest smile—like the one she was flashing him now. And she was a good listener—though he usually didn't have much to say. However, tonight, beneath the Parisian moonlight, he noticed her incredible beauty. How exactly had he missed it all this time?

"This is it!" Sylvie tugged on his arm. "We can take the photo here. It'll look amazing."

He stopped and glanced around. The Eiffel Tower was all lit up against the dark sky. So clichéd. And yet so utterly stunning.

"Stand right there." Sylvie pulled her phone from her sparkly black purse. "Turn to me."

And then he realized she was going to take his picture—all alone. Just like he was in life. The thought stole the smile from his face. He didn't want to be alone—at least for tonight.

Tonight he wanted Sylvie to be next to him. After all, she'd dropped everything to come with him on this trip. And he knew it hadn't been easy for her as a wedding planner to get her work done ahead of time and then show someone else what needed to be accomplished in her absence. Luckily for him, a wedding had been canceled, otherwise Sylvie wouldn't have been able to accompany him.

But she was here and she was captivating. It wasn't just him who noticed but everyone at the awards ceremony. Her black gown with the sparkly, strapless, fitted bodice was tapered at her tiny waist, and a plain, gauzy white material touched her hips and flowed to her ankles. And then the most delicate black heels showed off her painted toes.

She went from being a businesswoman in her smart tailored suits to a stunning siren who could turn all of the males' heads—his most especially. And it was making him quite uncomfortable. He wasn't sure what to say or do around her.

Because what he wanted to do now was pull her into his arms and kiss those very sexy, very tempting lips. But he resisted—just barely. They were friends. Nothing more. Even if she did look like some sort of goddess in that dress and that makeup that highlighted her alluring eyes, her high cheekbones and kissable lips. Wow!

She signaled for him to move to his right. "A

little more. Perfect." She held up her phone to snap a picture.

"Oh, no." In the glow of her smile, he felt his dismal mood begin to lift. "You have to come over here and have your picture taken, too."

Sylvie shook her head. "Not me. I didn't do anything special tonight. You're the man of the hour."

"But without you, I might not have entered." It was true. She'd nudged him into submitting his wine to the prestigious contest.

Was that a blush? He looked harder but it was too dark to be sure. Maybe it was just that he was starting to know her well enough to know his words would cause her cheeks to pinken.

Tonight hadn't been some small, local contest. This had been an international event with worldwide recognition. He honestly hadn't thought their small winery had any chance of winning against the big establishments. But Sylvie had insisted he would never know unless he entered. And so he'd decided he had nothing to lose and entered.

She snapped a picture. The flash lit up, blinding him for a moment.

"That's not fair," he said. "I want a picture, too."

"I'll send you a copy."

"No. That won't do. I want one of us together, so I'll have it to remember this night." It wasn't until the words were out of his mouth that hc realized how they might sound. Or maybe he was just being paranoid because he was having this very intense, undeniable attraction to her. His sister's friend—*his* friend.

He knew following this attraction through to its logical conclusion would be a mistake. Sylvie wasn't a one-night-stand kind of woman. She was a let's-get-to-know-each-other-fall-in-love-and-get-married type of woman. And that was the exact wrong type for him at this point in his life.

He stopped his rambling thoughts. What had gotten into him? He never allowed his thoughts to go in this direction with Sylvic. So why tonight? Was it being in Paris together? Was it one too many toasts to his winning success?

He latched on to the last thought and clung to it like it was a life preserver and he was a man adrift in a big, stormy sea. Or did he have it all wrong and Sylvie *was* his life preserver?

The next thing he knew, she was standing next to him. It was only natural to put his arm around her—for the picture, of course. But then she leaned into him, sending his heart racing.

Just ignore it. You've got this.

"Smile," he said—at least, he thought he said it. It was so hard to tell because he couldn't hear his thoughts over the echo of his heartbeat.

He snapped the picture. There. It was done.

But when he went to move his arm, she said, "No. Don't. Take one more."

There was a little voice in his head that said he should get while the getting was good, but that thought was drowned out by the thumping of his heart. It was just a picture. And she was just a friend.

He once more held the camera out in front of them. "Okay. Are you ready?"

When she didn't respond, he turned to look at her. It was the same moment that she turned her head to look at him. And with those stiletto heels, she was closer to his height.

When he thought back upon this moment, it would be the defining moment. This was when he should have turned away instead of staring deeply into her warm brown eyes that were so expressive. And right now they were saying that she wanted more from him than their platonic friendship. And so help him, so did he. So much more.

Her heart pitter-pattered.

Her breathing was soft and shallow.

Sylvie felt as though she was having an out-of-body experience. Maybe that was what she needed to tell herself in that moment to give her the courage to reach out to Enzo. Her hand cupped his freshly shaved cheek.

If she didn't do this now and quickly, she knew she would lose her courage. And though she'd been thinking about this for the longest time, if she didn't act now, she would never fulfill her wish. And the one thing she'd learned in her short life is that you had to grasp the happy moments because they were fleeting and few.

This was her happy moment. Enzo was the person who made her happy. And right now she felt so many intense emotions, she wasn't able to put a name to all the jumbled feelings zinging through her body.

But nothing was going to stop her from doing this one thing. She lifted up on her tiptoes. Even though her heels were high, they weren't enough for Sylvie to come face-to-face with him.

And then he was there, directly in front of her. And his mouth was just a breath away from her. An urge—or was it an impulse?—so strong, so swift, came over her. She was helpless to resist.

Not thinking through the consequences of her actions, she leaned forward, closing the distance. She pressed her lips to his. There was a distinct and swift intake of air on his part.

She'd surprised him? Really? She may be a virgin but that didn't mean she was totally naive. She'd seen the way he'd been looking at her tonight when he didn't think she was paying attention.

Her body trembled with nerves as her lips moved over his unmoving mouth.

No. Please. This can't end like this.

Inside, her heart was starting to crack. It had taken every bit of nerve to work up to this moment. She knew if she didn't make the first move, he never would.

And just when she thought he wasn't as into her as she'd thought, he reached out to her. His arm wrapped around her waist, pulling her to him. She followed his lead, letting her hands come to rest on his shoulders—his muscled shoulders gained from long hours of toiling the soil at the vineyard.

His lips moved over hers at a dizzying pace. Her heart beat so fast she thought it was going to pound its way out of her chest. She'd been kissed before but nothing like this. Those had been inexperienced schoolboys who'd only pretended they knew what they were doing, but Enzo, he knew exactly what he was doing. And she wanted him to show her more, much more.

Enzo pulled back. His breathing was ragged. He pressed his forehead to hers. "Sylvie, I… I—"

"Don't say it." She knew he was going to apologize for kissing her and it would ruin this moment—this very precious moment.

"But I shouldn't have let things get out of hand—"

"What if I wanted things to get out of hand?" Her gaze searched his. "I kissed you. Enzo, I've wanted to kiss you for the longest time. Tonight I finally worked up the courage."

Wow! Where had that come from? She never talked this boldly to men. Maybe that was why she didn't have a steady boyfriend—why she was still a virgin. In the past, she could blame her limited experience with men on caring for her ailing mother. But now it was all on her—what did or didn't happen was totally up to her.

She was tired of standing on the sidelines, watching her life rush past her. It was time to do what she wanted, instead of just dreaming about those things. It was time she took charge of her life.

And right now she wanted Enzo.

She trusted him more than anyone else in the world. These past few months they'd spent almost every day together. She knew him and he knew her. He was kind. He was thoughtful. And he had a big heart where his family was concerned.

And then there was his looks. Mmm…tall, dark and sexy didn't even begin to describe him. His dark eyes were mysterious and held a host of secrets that she longed to unravel. And his thick brown hair made her hands tingle with the impulse to comb her fingertips through it. And his mouth, well, she'd already proven it was most desirable.

For a moment Enzo didn't respond. His eyes registered his surprise at her forwardness. Part of her was proud of herself for speaking up. The other part of her was scared that he would let her down with a painful thump to her heart.

His gaze searched hers. "Sylvie, I'm in no position to start something serious. I—"

She placed a fingertip to those kissable lips. "I'm not asking you for anything permanent. I'm just asking you for the here and now. Let tomorrow take care of itself."

Hesitation showed in his eyes. "I don't want to hurt you."

The fact he cared that much meant a lot to her. And it was enough. Throughout the trials and tribulations of her life, she'd learned to be cautious with her heart.

She sent him a reassuring smile. "You won't hurt me. You've always been so sweet and kind."

Silence greeted her very honest words. All of this openness had her heart racing. What was she going to do if this all blew up in her face? After all, she was no temptress. She was not experienced in the ways of men. For all she knew, she could be making an utter fool of herself.

"Do you want to continue this back at the hotel?" His deep voice was thick and rich like the tiramisu dessert they'd indulged in at the dinner before the awards ceremony.

When her gaze met his, she saw desire burning in his eyes. Her insecurities were temporarily subdued. Her insides melted. Her core quivered with its own desire.

She didn't trust herself to speak. Instead, she lifted up on her tiptoes once more and pressed her lips to his. She deepened the kiss, opening her mouth to him, showing him that she didn't want this most exciting, most romantic night to end. In fact, this was just the beginning.

And then she pulled back. She laced her fingers with his and then started walking in the direction of their hotel. His thumb moved over the back of her hand. His roughened skin from working with his hands all day made his touch feel a little different, a little more exciting. Everything about Enzo was exciting.

The quick walk passed in silence. And then

they came to a stop in front of the first hotel room they came to. It happened to be hers. Her heart raced as anticipation pumped through her veins. At last, she was going to find out what all her friends were talking about when they mentioned their boyfriends and got that dreamy look in their eyes. Not that Enzo was her boyfriend. She wasn't sure what to call him because *friend* didn't begin to cover their increasingly complex relationship.

She turned to him and asked, "You haven't changed your mind, have you?"

Both of his dark brows rose high on his forehead. Had she said something wrong? Doubts circled in her mind. Her head lowered. His silence increased her rising anxiety. She worried her bottom lip. She'd done this all wrong—

He placed a finger beneath her chin and lifted until their gazes met. "Why would you think I've changed my mind? You're the most beautiful, most amazing woman I've ever met. I just can't believe you want me, too."

"I do." Her voice was so soft that she wasn't sure she'd actually vocalized the words, but there was a look of acknowledgment on his face.

How could he not know all this time that

she'd wanted him? She thought it was written all over her face every time she looked at him. It must be obvious she was utterly and totally inexperienced. She couldn't help but wonder why he'd want to make love to her when she didn't know what she was doing. She thought of asking him, but her mouth was dry and her mind was having trouble communicating with her mouth.

But luckily this time, she didn't have to do anything because it was Enzo who leaned down and pressed his lips to hers. His kiss, though gentle enough, was full of desire. It whipped up her pulse and stirred her own embers of desire.

Tonight she would become a woman in every sense of the word. And her friends would no longer be able to hold anything over her head. Tonight she would find out all about lovemaking with the most amazing man in the world.

CHAPTER ONE

Tuscany, six weeks later

HE HAD A SECRET.

A secret he'd shoved to the far recesses of his mind.

A secret he'd held on to for too long.

Enzo paced back and forth across the spacious balcony. A frown pulled at his face as a stress headache settled in his forehead and wrapped around his head, tightening like a vise.

He'd known for many years that one of the Bartolini siblings wasn't a true Bartolini by blood. His chest tightened just like it did every time he replayed the tumultuous events in his mind. The reason he'd never said anything—never admitted the painful truth—was that he thought he was the illegitimate sibling.

He raked his fingers through his hair as he blew out a breath. He'd totally made a mess of things. And after everything that had happened with his mother's journal and the reading of his parents' will, he still hadn't gotten his act together.

His mistakes continued to mount. Even though it had been weeks since the Paris trip, Enzo was still kicking himself for letting things get out of control with Sylvie. And rightly so. Sylvie had been a virgin. *A virgin.* The word echoed in his mind.

She should have saved that special moment for someone whom she loved. The evening should have included flowers and champagne as well as a bunch of other romantic platitudes.

Guilt settled on his shoulders like a big soggy cloak. Instead, the evening had been all about him and the vineyard. It should have been about her and how special she is. How had he missed all of this? He'd searched his memory, trying to recall if she'd told him that she was a virgin. But he was certain she hadn't mentioned it.

And yet, their night of passion had happened and now he could barely face her. He felt like she was expecting something from him. And yet, he didn't have anything to offer her. His life was a mess.

And to top it off, tomorrow was his birthday.

Nothing about this week felt festive. And that was fine by him. He wasn't in any mood to celebrate his birthday or anything else.

Enzo stood on the balcony of his family's grand estate, which had recently been remodeled into a boutique hotel. It was hard to believe that it had been less than a year since his parents stood in this very place. Now they were gone and with them went his illusion of the family he'd been a part of.

Since their deaths, the changes were falling like dominoes, one right after the next. Nothing was like it had been. Everyone was making life-changing decisions. And now it was his turn.

It should have been the biggest decision of his life. And yet, it felt predestined. The decision should have taken time—lots of time. It would have been surprising to make a momentous decision like this so quickly. However, this decision had been made for him before he even knew there was a question.

One evening was all it'd taken to change

everything. That wasn't much time at all in the grand scheme of things. However, he'd drug his heels about making it official.

And now, with his decision at last vocalized, the Monday-morning sun rose in the sky just as it had always done. It was oblivious to the monumental changes going on in Enzo's life. And so he went about life just as he had been doing. He'd already been out in the fields inspecting the vines. It wouldn't be long now and they'd be able to harvest the grapes.

His first season in sole charge of the vineyard and it was going to prove to be their biggest and best year. His father would have loved to see all their hard work come to fruition. If only that horrific car accident hadn't stolen both of Enzo's parents away.

If his parents were still here, Enzo's family wouldn't have been blown apart by a deep, dark secret that his parents had been harboring for many years. It was a secret Enzo had thought he knew the answer to. But when DNA results revealed his youngest sister, Gia, was not a Bartolini by blood but rather a result of their mother's affair, he'd been utterly floored.

He'd seen the way the news had stunned Gia

and ripped her heart apart. But he couldn't have been prouder of her when she pulled herself together and went in search of her biological father. Not everyone could do such a thing. He wasn't sure he could have done what she did…

"Enzo, I have the mail." Sylvie, the estate's wedding planner, stepped onto the balcony.

He didn't turn around. "I don't want to look at it now. Just toss it in the office." Then, realizing he'd forgotten his manners—manners his mother had instilled in him—he said, "Thank you."

Sylvie stepped up next to him. "You might want to see these two things."

Her words stirred his curiosity. "Why's that?"

"They're from your sisters."

A smile tugged at his lips. Through it all, they'd still remembered his birthday. When Sylvie held out two pieces of mail, he readily accepted them.

The first was a postcard. It was from the island of Lapri. The front of it had a picture of a dog licking gelato with the beach in the background. Okay, so a postcard wasn't exactly a birthday card, but it was the thought that counts. He flipped it over, already knowing it was from Gia.

Having a great time. The villa is almost remodeled. I'll have to find another house to work on. G

That was it? His gaze searched the card again. No birthday wishes. No *I miss you*. No *I'm coming back*. Not even a *Love, Gia*. Just a little note and an impersonal, unfeeling *G*.

His good mood deflated like a balloon stuck with a sharp needle. A big *whoosh* and his mood was back to its prior melancholy state of being.

Enzo blew out a deep sigh. This confirmed that their close-knit family was forever fractured. Nothing would ever be as it had been. If only he hadn't held on to that secret—the one he wasn't supposed to know anything about—maybe then things wouldn't be so different.

"Aren't you going to open the other one?" Sylvie's voice drew him from his thoughts. "It looks official. It has a crest on it and everything."

Enzo lifted the cream-colored envelope and saw the purple seal on the back. It was from his other sister Bianca. He noticed that the envelope was weighty, like there might be a card inside. A little smile played at the corners of his mouth. Bianca was always good at remembering his birthday.

He recalled the one time she'd planned a surprise for him. It was a birthday party in the garden. The only problem was she'd only invited her friends—her girlfriends. And most of them had crushes on him. Bianca had a good laugh, but he'd never been so glad for a party to end.

He slipped his finger under the flap—

"Stop!"

He hesitated and turned to Sylvie. "What?"

She wore a look of horror, as though he was about to destroy something sacred. "You can't just rip that open."

"Why not?" It was an envelope. Sure, it was of much finer quality, but still, it was an envelope. "If I don't open it, how will I know what's inside?"

"Wait. Don't move. I'll be right back." She rushed back inside the villa.

He thought about going ahead and opening it, but he didn't want to upset Sylvie. She was going to be upset enough when he told her his news. There was no need to make this day any worse. He just didn't know why Sylvie was making such a big fuss over an envelope.

A minute later she returned, holding up a silver letter opener. "Here you go."

He took the letter opener that was older than he was and handed down from his grandparents to his parents and now to him. The metal tip slipped easily through the fold and he yanked. The paper tore in a straight line. Nice and neat, just like Sylvie wanted.

He withdrew the card. As his gaze took in the words, he realized it wasn't a birthday card but rather an invitation. Neither sister had remembered his birthday.

"What is it?" Excitement rang out in Sylvie's voice.

He didn't want to discuss it. Instead, he wordlessly handed the invite to her.

She took it and began to read. Oohs and ahs accompanied each line she read. "This is amazing. You must be so excited to be invited to your sister's wedding. Can you believe you'll be related to a real-life prince?"

Enzo cleared his throat. "I don't care who

marries my sister as long as he makes her happy." By the raised brows on Sylvie's face, he realized his voice had been gruffer than he'd intended. "I'm sure Prince Leo will make her happy. She certainly seemed excited enough when she moved to Patazonia."

"Oh, she was." Sylvie wore a dreamy smile.

He didn't want to talk about his sister, especially not the new life she'd been thrust into by their parents' unreasonable will, which had pushed all three siblings to compete against each other for ownership of this estate. Maybe if it hadn't been for the unusual will and ridiculous requirement, his family would still be together—

He halted his thoughts. That wasn't the truth. It was his fault. He should have tried harder to protect his sisters—to keep them all together.

You're the big brother. You have to watch out for your sisters. Keep them safe.

His father's words echoed in his mind. How many times over the years had his father told him that? Too many times to count. And now when it was urgent for him to do just that, he'd failed them.

Not only had he failed his sisters but he was

also about to disappoint Sylvie. And just like his sisters, she wouldn't see this news coming.

What was going on?

As Sylvie continued to study the distinct frown on Enzo's face, the more confused she became. He'd been acting strange ever since he got home from the wine competition—which he'd won. But instead of being excited, he'd been moody and quiet. And worst of all, he'd pulled away from her.

Whereas they'd started off as friends, joking and laughing with each other, they now acted like mere acquaintances. Gone was the warm, easy companionship.

When he'd invited her to Paris, she'd thought it was the start of something serious between them. Boy had she been wrong. So very wrong.

Within a couple weeks of returning from Paris, everything looked dismal. Not only had Enzo put up a wall between them, but with his decision to close the boutique hotel, the wedding business was dwindling. People had been drawn in with the package deal. Now with just a wedding venue and no lodgings, well, the competition was drawing away business.

Maybe if she hadn't acted spontaneously in Paris—if she hadn't forced their relationship to the next level—she'd be able to convince Enzo to reopen the hotel. But with the mood he was in these days, that wasn't going to happen.

If it wasn't for that one unforgettable night, things would be different. Heat rushed to her cheeks when she recalled the night he'd won the prestigious competition. It had been a very special night for her, too. Perhaps they'd celebrated a little too much and then one thing led to another until she'd wound up in his arms all night long. She'd let herself believe he cared for her—like she cared for him.

But then they'd returned to Tuscany. It was like their passion had all been a steamy, stirring dream, but a dream nonetheless. And though that had been weeks ago, she was still trying to figure out what had happened.

They just needed to address the elephant in the room. The air needed clearing because she had important business to discuss with him. And this time she wouldn't let him come up with an excuse to walk away—like he'd done so many times before.

"Enzo—" she waited until she had his full

attention and then she continued "—we need to discuss the future of the wedding business. I have some ideas to go over with you."

This was it. This was further than she'd gotten in the past. She straightened her shoulders and met his gaze, letting him know she meant business. Would he stay this time and hear her out? Or would he make an excuse again?

When he started for the door, he said, "Maybe later. I need to get back to work."

In the past she'd let him escape. Maybe she should have spoken up before now. Maybe she shouldn't have let things drag on to this point. But it was so hard when the first time you make love and you think it was great—special even—and the guy thinks otherwise.

At first, she'd cried into her pillow at night. But time had helped soothe her wounded heart—or was it her pride? Perhaps a little of both. Either way, she wasn't going to be ignored. No one deserved that, not after what they'd shared.

She rushed over to the doorway before he could escape inside. When she stepped in front of him, his widened gaze settled on her.

"Sylvie, this isn't the time." His tone was gruff. "I have things to do."

She settled her hands on her hips. "Not before we talk."

He sighed. A moment of tense silence passed before he said, "Okay. What do you want to talk about?"

"You."

This got his attention. His gaze connected with hers, sending a jolt of awareness zinging through her body, but she refused to acknowledge it. Not now. Not like this.

"What about me?" His tone was cool and distant.

"I want to know why you've been acting different since we slept together—like we're strangers."

For a moment there was some sort of emotion in his eyes, but in a blink it was shuttered behind a wall of indifference. "I don't know what you mean."

Her back teeth ground together. He wasn't going to do this to her. During the years of caring for her mother, she'd learned to be a fighter—fighting to keep a roof over their heads, fighting to have her mother admitted to a new clinical trial, fighting to make their lives as normal as possible. Through it all, she'd learned how to speak up and not back down.

Frustration bubbled up within her. "Don't do this. Talk to me. I don't understand what went wrong. I… I thought we both wanted that night. Didn't we?"

He continued to stare at her. If he thought she was going to turn away, he had another think coming. She was the best starer in her primary school.

Then he let out a breath. His shoulders lowered just a bit, as though what had been holding him up had escaped in that breath. "I don't know what you want from me."

"How about the truth? Why have you been avoiding me?"

The silence returned. It dragged on so long that she was pretty certain he was never going to answer her—never going to tell her what she'd done wrong.

"Why didn't you tell me?" There was a note of accusation in his tone.

"Tell you?" She had no idea what he was talking about. "Tell you what?"

"That you were…you know."

"No, I don't know. Tell me."

His mouth pressed closed as his dark brows drew together into a formidable line. "Tell me that you were a virgin."

Her mouth opened to reply but no words would form as her mind raced with a million thoughts at once. Instead, she stood there with her mouth gaping open.

He was mad because she didn't make a big deal out of her virginity? Seriously? How in the world could he be mad about that? Realizing that her mouth was still gaping open, she promptly closed it.

Enzo continued to stare at her like he really expected her to answer him. She didn't know what sort of answer he expected. Or why she had to explain herself.

"I… I didn't know my virginity needed to be stated before we made love. Would it really have made a difference?"

"Of course it would have." He raked his fingers through his thick, dark hair, sending the short strands scattering. When his gaze met hers this time, there was an intensity there that she'd never seen before. "How could you think otherwise?"

"Because I wasn't thinking about it when we were standing in front of the Eiffel Tower. All I was thinking about was you." Intense heat rushed to her face upon realizing that she'd said too much.

"Didn't you think I deserved to know?"

"No." Was that selfish of her? She didn't think so. It's not like any of this really affected him or their time together. There was something else going on here—something he wasn't telling her.

Then he sighed. The lines on his handsome face smoothed. He turned away from her. He moved to the balustrade and then rested his forearms on the rail.

"I'm sorry," he said. Though with him turned away from her, she had to strain to hear his words. "I shouldn't have said that. I just have a lot on my mind."

She wanted to ask if he was also sorry that they'd slept together, but she held back the words—but barely. At least they were getting somewhere. Now, if she could just keep him talking.

"Is it your sisters?" She'd known ever since she'd come to live and work at the Bartolini estate that his parents' sudden deaths had caused not just a ripple through his life but a tsunami of pain that had shaken each Bartolini sibling to the very core.

"Yes. No. Not really." There was anguish in his voice. Whatever was bothering him went deep, very deep.

She moved to stand next to him at the rail. The scene of the rolling hills of the vineyard was stunning and usually captivated her attention, but right now she was fully focused on Enzo.

Sylvie placed a hand on his arm. "You know you can talk to me about anything?"

He turned his head to look at her and then turned away. "Not about this."

She stifled a sigh. Had they really come full circle? "Is this about Paris?"

"Yes. And no."

She normally considered herself a patient person. After all, to be a good wedding planner, you needed to remain calm at all times, even when the bride was having an utter meltdown and blaming the whole world. Right now Sylvie would give anything to be dealing with a nervous bride and not a stubborn Enzo.

Sylvie straightened her shoulders. She wasn't backing off. "You need to tell me what's on your mind because this guessing game isn't working for me. If you're mad about me being a virgin—"

"No. It's not that. And I wasn't mad that you were a virgin. I was mad that I didn't know." He turned to her. Pain evident in his eyes. "If I had known, I would have…" He paused. "I would have backed away."

"Why? Do you have a thing against virgins?"

"No. Of course not." He shook his head. "But you should have shared that moment with someone special—someone you love."

"Oh." This time she was the one who glanced away. Heat licked at her cheeks.

CHAPTER TWO

HE WAS MUCKING up this conversation. Royally.

And worst of all, he was hurting Sylvie.

Enzo inwardly groaned. She had a heart of gold and deserved someone better than him. She should have a man who had it all together. Someone who could look at her like she'd hung the stars.

That was why he'd been keeping his distance. He'd suspected before they flew to Paris that she might have some feelings for him, but other times he was certain he was just reading more into their friendship than was there.

And then she'd kissed him in front of the Eiffel Tower. Was it awful of him to admit that he hadn't seen it coming? Not at all.

Of course, that might have been because he'd just had one of the most important conversations of his life. There had been an offer to buy Barto Vineyard as well as the entire estate.

Now, of course, this hadn't been the first

offer for the estate. Over the years, his father had had plenty of inquiries. All of which his father had immediately dismissed. To his father, this place—this land—it was in his soul. He needed it as much as he needed his next breath.

However, Enzo now saw the estate in a much different view. This may be where his family had started, but it was also where that family had splintered apart. The secrets that were kept within the stone walls of the villa all these years were like poison, killing the family that he'd once known.

Now one sister lived in Patazonia and was renouncing her Italian citizenship in order to become a princess. And his other sister had left the mainland to live on a Mediterranean island—far from home. It was though his sisters couldn't wait to get as far away from this place as they could. And maybe they were right.

Maybe it was time for him to move on—time for him to forge a new life somewhere far from Tuscany and all the memories tied up in this place.

And that was why he hadn't immediately dismissed the offer to buy the estate. But he hadn't accepted the offer, either. He'd needed time to think it over. And that was what he'd been doing ever since they'd returned from Paris. Thinking. And thinking. And thinking some more.

And at last, he'd come to a decision.

Not an easy decision. Not that he'd expect something this big, this profound, to be made easily. But now that he solely owned the estate by default—as both of his sisters had found their happiness elsewhere—the decision was solely his to make.

And now it was time to share the news with Sylvie.

He glanced over at her, knowing how this was going to crush her. His chest tightened. "Sylvie, there's something I need to tell you."

The color leeched from her face. "What is it?"

She was so pale now that he was worried about her. "Do you feel all right?"

"The news. What is it?"

He hesitated. "Maybe we should sit down."

"No. I'm fine right here. What is it you wanted to tell me?"

He drew in a deep breath and then let it out. It

didn't matter how long he put this off; it wasn't going to get easier for either of them. It was best just to get it over with as quickly as possible. "I've agreed to sell the estate."

If it was possible for her face to grow paler, it most definitely had. Even her normally glossy pink lips were devoid of gloss this morning and had lost their color.

"You did what?" Her voice faded with each word.

And then she swayed.

He moved, his arms wrapping around her. Instinctively, he pulled her to him. "I've got you."

She pressed her hands to his chest. "I'm fine. Let me go."

He guided her over to one of the chairs at a table on the terrace. "Can I get you anything?"

She shook her head. "Stop fussing. I'm fine."

"No, you're not. You almost passed out over there. Are you sick?"

Again, she shook her head. "I'm not sick. I keep telling you, I'm fine."

"People that are fine don't pass out."

"I didn't pass out."

"Okay, then you almost passed out. I'm not

letting this go until you tell me what's going on. Is it the news?"

She shrugged. "I didn't eat breakfast this morning and I went for a run."

"On an empty stomach?" No wonder she'd almost passcd out.

She shrugged once more. "When?"

"What?"

"When is the estate being sold?"

"I don't know. I just made the call this morning. We have to work out the details. Nothing has been fully decided."

She didn't say anything to that. She got to her feet and quietly walked away, leaving him feeling worse than he had before.

He thought she would yell at him—blame him for ruining her business. Anything would have been better than the silent treatment. Though he supposed he deserved it because ever since Paris he'd been quiet, too—trying to figure out the right thing to do for his family and for himself.

But was it the right thing for Sylvie?

His proclamation had stunned her.

The next morning Sylvie sat behind her desk

in the guesthouse. She didn't feel as though she'd accomplished a thing that morning. At least nothing that was on her to-do list.

She'd spent most of yesterday in this little cottage on the estate. And she intended to do the same today. She told herself it was because she had a lot of work to do, but the real reason was that she was avoiding Enzo.

The cottage was quiet and out of the way. It was used in part for wedding services, from choosing a gown, to dress fittings, to choosing decorations and everything else. Princess Bianca—well, she wasn't officially a princess until Christmas—had invested most of the income from the weddings back into the business, building it up. Now the business was amazing. And Sylvie felt as though she had a dream job, but like with all dreams, it was coming to an end.

Her stomach felt as though it was on the high seas, swaying this way and that. As such, her appetite was nonexistent.

All the while her mind was on Enzo. How could he sell the estate? This was the same place he'd competed with his sisters over in order to claim ownership. And now he just suddenly changed his mind? She didn't understand.

It also meant she would once again be homeless. Tears rushed to her eyes but she blinked them away.

She never used to be emotional. She couldn't afford to be when she'd had to care for her mother. She'd had to be the strong one. Her mother had needed her to lean on.

She'd been calm and collected when, after her mother's death, the bank had repossessed the small house she'd grown up in. With only part-time work so she could care for her mother, she hadn't been able to keep up with the mortgage payments.

For a time, she'd been on her own with nothing more than what she could carry. It had been horrible but not as bad as losing her mother and knowing that she was all alone in this world, after having lost her father in a horrific accident when she was just a baby.

But Enzo's circumstances were different than hers. He had not only a home but also a family to rely on. Whether he was willing to acknowledge it or not, this estate was his destiny. The Barto Vineyard was as much a part of him as the blood flowing through his veins. But how did she get him to see this?

There was a knock at the door. Before she could get up, she heard the door creak open.

"Sylvie?" It was Enzo. "Sylvie, are you in here?"

"In the office."

Her empty stomach shivered with nerves. What did he want to talk about now? She didn't know what to say to change his mind about the sale.

Enzo stepped into the office. His tall stature and broad shoulders seemed to fill the room, making the office feel much smaller than it truly was. He looked around the room, never letting his gaze rest on her. His intent on taking in everything in the office made it seem like he'd never been in here before, but the truth was he'd been in the office countless times.

When the silence turned uncomfortable, Sylvie asked, "Was there something you needed?"

He hitched his thumbs in the corners of his jean pockets and ducked his head. "I wanted to say I was sorry for how I handled things yesterday."

"You mean springing it on me that I've lost not only my home but also my business, too?"

He kept his gaze down toward the floor as he nodded. "Don't worry. I plan to help you out."

"Help me out?" She didn't like the sound of that. She wasn't a charity case. She'd already had to accept the help of others after her mother passed on. That had been so hard to do. She wasn't going to do that again. She had worked hard to put away some savings. It would tide her over until she came up with another job.

He nodded and then his gaze met hers. "You just have to tell me where you want to settle and I'll make sure you have a place to live. If you want, I can set you up with your own wedding business."

Her mouth gaped. Realizing she must look like a guppy, she pressed her lips together as she attempted to gather her scattered thoughts.

"Why?" When he sent her a puzzled look, she elaborated on her thought. "Why would you do something like that? It's so…so generous."

He rubbed the back of his neck. "Because it's

my fault you're losing your place to live and work. It seems like the only right thing to do."

She seized upon that last part of his explanation. "The right thing to do? So you're doing this out of some sense of obligation?"

"Well, yes."

That was what she figured. He was a man driven by his sense of duty and obligation. She didn't want to be one of his obligations. "That won't be necessary. You don't owe me anything—"

"Of course I do—"

"No, you don't." She stood so he didn't have quite such a height advantage over her. "I'm not part of your family. There's no reason for you to feel obligated where I'm concerned. I…" She almost mentioned that she took care of not only herself but also her mother, but decided against bringing it up. There was a lot she still hadn't shared with him because she hadn't wanted to scare him off with all her heavy baggage. "I can take care of myself."

A frown settled on his handsome face. "Of course you can. I didn't mean to imply otherwise. But I just feel bad about you moving here all the way from Patazonia and already the business is shutting down. That's not fair."

"Life isn't fair. I learned that a long time ago."

Like when her mother struggled with three jobs to keep a roof over their heads when Sylvie was young. Her mother had been a seamstress, one of the best in the land, but when business had dropped off because people started buying clothes over the internet, her mother picked up cleaning jobs to help balance the budget.

"Sylvie, what are you talking about?"

She shook her head. "It's nothing." He eyed her as though trying to read the truth in her eyes. Worried he'd see too much, she glanced away. It was time to change the subject away from her. She lifted her gaze once more. "Are you sure this is what you want to do?"

"What? Help you? Of course I am."

She shook her head. "No. I mean sell this place."

This time it was his turn to glance away. "I'm certain."

"But just months ago you were determined to beat both of your sisters and win ownership of the villa, the vineyard—the entire estate. How can you change your mind so quickly?"

His brows gathered in a firm line and when his gaze landed on her, it was dark and stormy. "Because this isn't the place it used to be. It's broken and tarnished. It's best for me and my sisters to put it in our rearview mirrors and keep moving forward."

Ouch! She had no idea he was harboring such hostilities regarding his childhood home. But something told her selling the estate wouldn't resolve the turmoil going on inside him. It went far deeper than grapevines and a place to lay his head at night.

"But what will you do?" she asked. "Where will you go?"

"I don't know. Maybe back to Paris. I have a standing invitation to go work at a prestigious vineyard there."

"But it won't be your vineyard." She'd seen the pride he took in the grapes at the Barto Vineyard. Even though it was an enormous vineyard with many employees, Enzo made sure to take part in all facets of the operation. "It won't have your family name on the wine."

His dark gaze was unreadable in that moment. "Maybe that's for the best. After everything that happened here this year, it is best to close the door on all of this."

It was then that Sylvie realized how big of a challenge she'd set for herself in changing his mind about remaining here. But she wasn't a quitter. She was a fighter. It was one of the last things her mother told her.

Never give up on life. Keep fighting for what's most important.

And right now Enzo's heritage was at stake as well as her business. She was as certain as she was standing here that he would regret parting with this land as much as she would regret not fighting to keep her home and occupation.

"I have to go," he said. "We'll talk more about this later."

Sylvie tried to think of a reason for him to stay. She glanced down at her desktop and her gaze landed on her calendar. "Wait." When he paused at the doorway and turned back to her, she said, "We need to talk about the sale. I need to know what weddings to work on relocating to a new venue."

He frowned. "I don't know. Nothing is official. The buyer is flying in two weeks from now to take a tour of the grounds."

"He's buying a place he's never seen?" Who did such a thing?

"He's been here for a wedding. And he's enjoyed the wine for many years. He says he's getting older now and is ready to settle down."

"How is running a vineyard settling down?"

Enzo shrugged. He worked from sunrise until sunset and always had more than he could get done in one day. "Not my problem."

"Can we go over my calendar?" she asked.

Enzo checked his wristwatch. "Not now. I have to meet up with Vito. We're having problems locating a replacement part for one of our tanks. Maybe later."

He already had one foot out the door when she thought of how she could gain more of his time. "How about dinner?"

He paused once more. "I can't eat until late."

"No problem. It'll give me a chance to throw something together." She wasn't sure what it would be but suddenly her appetite was starting to come back.

"Okay. If you're sure."

"I'm positive."

When he was gone, Sylvie worked to finish up the last of her urgent admin. The rest could wait until later. Right now she had something important on her mind—saving the estate. She had two weeks to convince Enzo that this was where he was meant to be. But how could she do it?

CHAPTER THREE

INSTEAD OF THINGS getting better, they were getting worse.

And it wasn't just the broken equipment in the winery.

Enzo had been grouchy with Sylvie and he hadn't meant to be. In fact, that was the very opposite of how he meant to act around her. Until that unforgettable night in Paris, she had been one of his closest friends.

Even though he had been busy doing everything he could to market his wine to new stores and foreign vendors, he always made time for her. Sylvie's smile was contagious and lightened his darkest days. Meeting up with her had always been the highlight of his day. Then he'd gone and mucked everything up.

Why hadn't he just been a gentleman and walked away after she'd kissed him? Because he couldn't. The magnetic pull between them had been something he'd never felt before.

And that night in Paris, wow. That night had been amazing. He still thought of it when he was alone in bed and sleep was evading him, as it did often these days.

The question was how did he get things back on track with Sylvie? He missed their friendship, but every time he was around her, words didn't come out the way he meant them to. And now when she looked at him, he felt even guiltier not only for the night in Paris but also for now taking her home and job. If only she'd let him help her get resettled somewhere else, he would feel better. In fact, he intended to talk to her about it tonight at the dinner she'd insisted on preparing.

He checked the time. It was almost eight. How did it get to be so late? He knew he better head up to the guesthouse before she thought he'd forgotten about dinner. The last thing he needed was to make things even worse between them. They were bad enough already.

And so he set off for the guesthouse where Sylvie was now living and working. He could fix things. He wouldn't give up until she listened to reason.

As he neared the guesthouse, his thoughts

turned to its prior resident. His youngest sister, Gia, had stayed here after their parents had died. Only she hadn't stayed here long. It seemed to him that she couldn't get away from the estate fast enough, first to find her biological father, who turned out to be a total and utter jerk, and then finally to move permanently to the island of Lapri with some guy she barely knew. But who was he to judge?

He'd believed everything his parents had told them without question. And when he'd overheard something that conflicted with his illusion of the perfect family, he dismissed it as a figment of his imagination. He'd failed his sisters. And he'd failed himself.

Enzo stepped up to the door of the guesthouse and rapped his knuckles on the heavy wood. When a few moments passed and Sylvie hadn't answered, he knocked louder. Still nothing. He moved to the side of the door and peered inside the window. It was dark in the front room. He figured she was in the kitchen at the back of the little house and hadn't heard him.

He walked to the back door and knocked. Still, there was no answer. What was up with that? He searched his memory and was certain she'd invited him to dinner tonight. He backed up and noticed there were no lights on back here, either. Was it possible he'd gotten his wires crossed? Had she meant the main house?

Not wanting her to know just how distracted he was these days, his pride refused to allow him to text her. He'd just walk up to the main house and pretend that was where he'd intended to go all along.

However, when he reached the back of the villa, it was dark inside, too. How could that be? Maybe he really had misconstrued what she'd told him.

Through the window in the door, he noticed the soft glow of the small light over the big farmhouse sink—his mother had always left on a light for his father when he'd worked late in the fields. As Enzo grasped the brass doorknob of the kitchen door, he gave himself a mental jerk. He tried not to think about his parents. Every time he did, his mood went south. That wouldn't be fair to Sylvie, who had gone out of her way to make him dinner. At least he thought she had.

He pushed the door open and stepped inside. He moved to the kitchen and flipped on the lights. The kitchen was spiffed up and as he inhaled, he definitely detected some basil and tomato sauce. He had a feeling he was on to something.

As it was a bit chilly outside that evening, he was certain Sylvie wasn't planning a terrace dinner. Perhaps she'd decided to utilize the dining room in order to use the long table to spread out her paperwork that she wanted to go over with him.

He started in that direction. However, when the doorway to the dining room came into sight, he noticed the door was almost closed while a flicker of soft light shone through the crack. Sylvie had planned a candlelight dinner for him?

As soon as the thought came to him, he dismissed it. He'd ruined any chance of anything romantic between them. Not that he was interested in starting a relationship. In fact, that was the last thing he wanted.

His personal life was a disaster. He might have won full ownership of the Bartolini estate but he'd lost what made it special—his family. In truth, he hadn't even won control of it. He'd won out of default. His sisters didn't want the place. They'd rather move far away and start over. Not that he could blame them after the way their lives had imploded upon finding their mother's journal.

But he wasn't going to think about that now. Right now he needed to make sure Sylvie hadn't gotten the wrong idea about tonight's dinner.

He pushed the door open. There was a single candle lit in the vast room. He squinted into the darkness. "Sylvie?"

The lights flicked on, momentarily blinding him.

"Surprise!" It wasn't just Sylvie's voice but a whole host of voices.

When his sight adjusted, he glanced around. Crowded into the dining room were all the workers from the vineyard as well as friends and neighbors. And then his gaze rested on Sylvie.

His jaw muscles tightened. He didn't want to celebrate his birthday. Not at all.

But everyone looked at him with a big smile on their faces and expectation in their eyes.

He was certain they all had better things to do with their time, but they'd taken time out of their lives to come here to celebrate his birthday. They didn't know that this year of all years he didn't have the heart to celebrate.

Still, he forced a smile to his face. Many of these people had worked for his family for decades. He owed them more than a fake smile, but it was the most he could do at this particular moment.

And then he was swallowed up in the moment. People were shaking his hand, clapping him on the back and wishing him a happy birthday.

What they didn't know and what he didn't tell them was that they would never come together like this again. And the vineyard workers would be losing their jobs in the near future, when the new owner took over.

Until this point, Enzo had refused to let himself acknowledge this very obvious—very painful fact. He knew if he was to consider it, he might very well back away from the offer. And then what? He remained here?

He didn't want to think about the past and wonder what else their parents had lied to them about. He wanted to do what his sisters had done and turn his back on this place.

Of all the people here this evening, he noticed that his sisters weren't among the guests. Not that he would expect them to drop everything in their very busy lives and travel here for his thirty-second birthday. But they'd never not remembered to give him a card. No matter where they were in their lives or in the world, they always remembered each other's birthdays. Until now.

"Great party, huh?"

Enzo glanced to his right. "Yeah."

Next to him stood his right-hand man, Vito. He had also been his father's second-in-command. His father and Vito had grown up together. But looking at Vito now, the only thing betraying his true age was his silver hair and mustache. Other than that, the man didn't look old enough to have grown children, nor did he act as though his first grandchild was on the way. He was a man with an abundance of energy and a smile for most anyone.

"It's too bad your parents aren't here to share this with you," Vito said. "They'd love it."

Enzo didn't want to discuss them. He had

too many mixed emotions where they were concerned.

"Did you get something to eat?" Enzo asked.

"I was headed that way. I just wanted to wish you a happy birthday." He extended his hand. They shook before sharing a quick one-armed hug. And then Vito moved toward the food.

The fact Sylvie went to so much trouble for him should have touched him—touched him deeply. And it did. But there was also another feeling nagging at him. Guilt. A huge case of it.

Why had she gone to such trouble for him? He didn't deserve it. He had let his frustrations show around her and that wasn't good. He could do better where Sylvie was concerned. He would do better.

There were meats and cheeses. A fruit platter took up a large portion of the table. Pasta was heaped in a large bowl with oil, olives, fresh diced tomatoes and herbs. There was enough food here to feed a small army. And as good as it all looked and smelled, he didn't have an appetite.

"Where's your plate?" Sylvie asked once the crowd thinned out around him.

"I…uh…didn't have a chance to get anything." He hoped she'd drop the subject, but he knew her well enough to know she'd push until he ate something.

"Then let's get you something." She reached for a plate and handed it to him. "Fill it up before the food is all gone."

If he had to eat, she did, too. "Where's your food?"

"I haven't had a chance to get some, either. So why don't we get some together?" She smiled at him. How was it possible that someone's smile could be so bright it warmed a spot in his chest?

He grabbed a plate for Sylvie and handed it to her. "Lead the way."

And so she did, helping him fill his plate until there was absolutely no room left. "How am I supposed to eat all of this?"

"You've worked hard all day. And those are all your favorites. I'm sure you'll find a way."

It was then that he stared down at the plate. She was right. These were all his favorites. "You did this, didn't you?"

She shrugged as she added some fresh fruit to her plate. "I just remembered. And I might have texted Bianca."

He smiled—his first smile of the day. "I'm not so sure how I feel about you and my sister being such good friends."

"Are you afraid I'll learn all of your secrets?"

Her innocent words struck far too close to home. "I don't know what you're talking about."

The smile slipped from her face. "Doesn't everyone have things they are holding back?"

He didn't want to have this conversation. Not at all. "Let's sit down and eat."

As they made their way to a couple of empty chairs, he rolled around her words in his mind. Was she referring to his family's secrets? Because he was certain she didn't know his secret. Or was she referring to her own?

Once they were seated, his curiosity was piqued. "Are you saying you're a woman of mystery?"

She arched a brow. "Would you like that?"

He pursed his lips together. There were still so many things about Sylvie that he didn't know. And he couldn't help but think he wanted to know everything about her. But now that he'd decided to sell the estate, she would be leaving here. Maybe not today. Maybe not tomorrow. But soon. Too soon.

It was best to let the subject drop. “What I’d like is to enjoy this food because there’s this great big cake with my name on it.”

Sylvie smiled. “You saw that?”

“How could I miss it? It’s huge and in the center of the table. How did you get the bakery to make it so quickly? Or did you have this party planned for a long time?”

“Actually, I didn’t realize it was your birthday until yesterday when I saw a notation on my day planner. There wasn’t any time to order a cake so I made it—”

“You baked me a birthday cake?”

She shrugged. “Kind of.”

“I don’t understand. You baked it or you didn’t?”

“It’s a box cake. Actually, it’s four boxes. I wanted to make sure there was enough for everyone.”

“Box or not, you’re the first person aside from my mother to ever bake me a cake.” The gesture touched him more profoundly than it should have. He leaned over to her. He was so tempted to reach out and turn her head toward him so he could press his lips to hers. The thought was so very, very tempting.

But not wanting to ruin this moment, he pressed a kiss to her cheek instead. "Thank you, for all of this."

Color filled her cheeks. "You're welcome."

And then before she could eat her food, she was called away to the kitchen. He wanted to go after her—to offer his help with whatever it might be. But he knew he couldn't push this thing between them—this second chance at a friendship.

"She's certainly something, isn't she?"

Enzo glanced up to find Vito standing there, smiling. "Excuse me?"

"Sylvie, she did all of this for you. You're one lucky man to have her in your life."

"She's not in my life." The statement came out with more force than he'd meant.

Vito's bushy brows rose high on his forehead. "Really? I thought you two were a couple."

Enzo gave a firm shake of his head. He cleared his throat. "We're just friends." Not wanting to continue this discussion, he said, "Excuse me. I need to go check on something."

As Enzo walked away, he couldn't stop

thinking about what Vito had said. There was still a part of him that wished Vito was right. But he had absolutely nothing to offer her.

His life was in turmoil. He wasn't even sure where he was going to live once the estate was sold. And then there was the fact he didn't deserve to have Sylvie in his life. He didn't want to fail her like he'd failed his sisters.

CHAPTER FOUR

THERE WAS A PEP to his step.

This was going to be a good day.

Enzo had slept well for the first time in forever. He tried to tell himself it was exhaustion that had let him slumber. But he wasn't that good of a liar. He knew it was the engaging party last night. And Sylvie.

She was such a remarkable woman. He had no idea she'd been planning a surprise party. And she'd made sure to invite everyone who worked at the vineyard as well as the neighbors. It had been so thoughtful—so sweet.

Some man was going to be very fortunate to marry her. She would make a loving wife. Not to mention a wonderful mother. The vision of her holding a baby in her arms filled his mind. The baby would be a little girl and she'd be the spitting image of her mother. A smile tugged at the corners of his mouth.

Then the image morphed as he envisioned

Sylvie laughing at something. A man moved next to her, placing an arm around her waist and pulling her gently to his side. She melted into him. The love in her eyes—

Enzo's thoughts screeched to a halt. The smile that had been playing on his lips turned to a distinctive frown. Not that he had any claim over Sylvie. They may have shared a night—a special night—but it was over. And he wanted her to be happy. He just didn't want to think about her being happy with someone else.

"Enzo, are you out here?" Sylvie's voice was carried on the morning breeze.

It was though his thoughts of her had drawn her to him. Of course, that was silly. Things like that didn't happen.

"I'm over here." He took a sip of his quickly cooling coffee and then he turned to her.

"Good morning." She sent him a smile.

Was it just him or did she look a bit on the pale side? It was probably the party last night. It had been hugely successful, but it had to have been a lot for her to set up so quickly. And then it had run late into the evening.

He suddenly felt bad for not ending the party

sooner. But after he'd eaten the delicious food and amazing cake Sylvie had baked, which he didn't believe could have come out of a box, he'd had a renewed energy. He'd made his way around the room talking with everyone who took time out of their busy lives to show up.

And gifts. There were gifts for him. A smile tugged at his lips, knowing people cared that much. There were books, wine from competitors, which were gag gifts, a wall hanging and more. It had been an amazing night. And it was all thanks to Sylvie. Sweet, sweet Sylvie.

He moved toward her and pulled out a chair from the table. "Here. Have a seat." When surprise registered in her eyes, he added, "You must be tired after all you did yesterday."

She hesitated then she sat. "Just a little tired. Although, I have to admit I was asleep last night as soon as my head hit the pillow."

"I bet. You really went above and beyond." And then he realized to his horror that he'd been so caught off guard last night that he hadn't thanked her. At least, he couldn't remember doing it. He sat next to her. "Thank you so much for the party. No one has ever thrown me a surprise party."

A smile lit up her face. "You're welcome. But it wasn't just me. Everyone chipped in and helped."

"But it was your idea and that cake, it was so good. I wanted to have some for breakfast but I couldn't find where you hid it."

"I… I didn't hide it." The smile slipped from her face. "I'm sorry. It's all gone."

"I'm not surprised. It was delicious."

"I can bake you another one."

"Are you kidding?" When he saw the serious look on her face, he said, "I don't want you to go to all of that trouble."

"I would."

"I know you would. And I really appreciate it—appreciate you." Now, what had he gone and added that last part for? It sounded too intimate. Too much like they were involved. Or maybe he was overthinking things. "Let me get you some coffee—"

"No." When he turned to her, certain he hadn't heard her right, she said, "I… I'll get some later."

"Later? Since when don't you drink coffee as soon as you wake up?"

She shrugged. "I think I've been drinking

too much of it. My stomach has been bothering me. So I'm taking a break."

"Maybe you're getting sick."

She shook her head. "I feel fine otherwise."

His gaze searched hers. What was going on with her? Maybe she'd overdone it yesterday. Or maybe it was stress over the pending sale of the estate.

Buzz. Buzz.

His phone vibrated in his pocket. He didn't want to be interrupted now. He wanted to make sure nothing serious was going on with Sylvie. But when he checked his caller ID, he couldn't not answer it.

"Happy birthday," Bianca said.

Gia echoed her words.

"You're both on here?"

"Yes," Bianca said. "We feel awful about missing your birthday."

"It's okay." It wasn't, but his pride refused to let him make a big deal of this. "No big deal—"

"Yes, it is," Gia said. "We didn't mean to miss your big day."

"But we have something special planned for you." A giddiness filled Bianca's voice.

That didn't sound good. His sisters and surprises could be a dangerous combination. "You don't have to do anything special. I'm fine."

"Of course we do. Mamma would expect us to do something," Gia said.

Silence filled the phone line. He knew that everyone was thinking of their parents and missing them. But at least his sisters had the strength to move on. He had to do that now, too—get away from all of the memories.

Still, he knew his sisters would keep going on about making a big deal out of his birthday unless he gave them a reason not to. "In fact, Sylvie—" he lifted his gaze, finding that she'd left the veranda, probably to give him some privacy "—planned a big surprise party."

Both of his sisters gushed at once and then they started pummeling him with questions about who was there and what had happened during the party. But it was the last question that he stumbled on. Was he involved with Sylvie?

The word *no* rushed to the back of his mouth, but then it stuck there. Why was he hesitating? They weren't involved. Not since Paris.

"Enzo, are you still there?" Bianca asked.

"He just doesn't want us to know what we've

suspected all along—he's totally into Sylvie." Gia's voice was gleeful.

"Stop." His voice came out gruffer than he'd intended. He didn't need his sisters ganging up on him right now—and certainly not about Sylvie.

"Woah!" Gia said. "Did we hit a nerve?"

"Gia," Bianca said, "I think we better leave it alone."

He knew he needed a distraction. And boy, did he have a huge distraction. He'd been putting off telling his sisters that he was selling the estate. He wasn't sure how they would take the news. The last thing in the world he wanted to do was cause them more pain. Still, they had moved on with their lives. Would the sale be an issue for them? Regardless, he needed to tell them now—before things progressed with the sale.

Enzo swallowed hard. "There's something I need to tell you both."

"I know," Bianca said, "you're getting married."

Gia gasped.

"What? No." He shook his head. "Where do you two come up with this stuff?"

"Well," Gia said, "you are getting older—"

"Gia," Bianca said, "it was a rhetorical question."

"Oh."

He smiled and shook his head. Maybe not everything had changed. His sisters were still acting like the fun, loving sisters he remembered back before the car accident upended all their lives in ways they never could have imagined.

"Okay, you two. I'm not getting married." The smile faded from his face. "But I do have something very serious to tell you."

An ominous silence fell over them.

"Are…are you sick?" Gia asked.

"Not that serious," he said. This was going all sorts of wrong. He just needed to say it and get it over with. "I'm selling the estate."

"What?" came the collective response.

He gave them a moment to get past the initial shock. He cleared his throat. "When I was in Paris, I was made an offer I can't turn down."

"But you competed against us in order to win the estate," Gia said.

"We thought you wanted it," Bianca said. "What about the vineyard?"

"What about our family home?" Gia's voice held disbelief.

He hadn't been sure how they would take the news, but he didn't think he'd have to defend himself. "Seeing as both of you have moved away—far away—I didn't think you'd care what happened to the estate."

"We care," Gia said.

Another strained silence filled the line.

"But we care about you more," Bianca said.

"Bianca?" Gia said. "You surely can't want to part with our childhood home."

"What I want and for that matter what you want, doesn't matter. We picked our futures. It's time to let our brother do what's right for him."

He should say something, anything, but he wasn't sure what that should be. He loved his sisters and he didn't want to do anything to upset them. Would they understand that he just couldn't stay here? He couldn't have a daily reminder of his failures in life.

"I'm sorry," Gia said. "Bianca's right. You were always there for us. We'll support whatever decision you make. But are you really sure you want to do this?"

This time there was no hesitation. “I’m sure.”

“But where will you go?”

“What will you do?”

His sisters peppered him with questions and though he had work to do, he indulged them. After all, they were taking this news really well. And if answering all their questions—questions that didn’t pertain to Sylvie—made them feel better, he could do that for them.

By the time he hung up the phone, an entire hour had passed. Before he headed to the vineyard, he wanted to say something to Sylvie. He found her in the kitchen, finishing a glass of fresh-squeezed *spremuta* and a roll with butter and jam. He was relieved to see the color in her cheeks and that she had an appetite.

“Sorry about that,” he said. “It was my sisters.”

“No problem. I just wanted to give you some space.” She placed her plate and juice glass in the sink. “And now I have to finalize some details for a wedding this weekend.”

“Ah, sure. I need to get to work, too.”

“I’ll talk to you later.”

With that, she was gone and he was left alone with his thoughts. His sisters said they were okay with the sale, but he had to wonder if that was the truth. And Sylvie was being so nice to him—too nice. What was up with that?

CHAPTER FIVE

SO WHAT HAD his sisters said?

Sylvie was dying to know if he'd told them about the sale of the estate, but she resisted questioning him because it wasn't her business. But that didn't keep her from wondering if they thought it was as big a mistake as she did. Would they be her allies?

Well, obviously not. Because there was no way she was going to wedge herself between the siblings—even if Bianca was a friend, a good friend. No, this was a battle she was going to have to wage on her own.

And it didn't help that Enzo kept doing one thing after another to surprise her—like at the party last night. In the beginning, he hadn't been overly enthused by it. In fact, she wasn't even sure if he'd stay for it. But as time went by, he started to eat the food, talk to the guests, and by the end of the evening he was laughing and smiling. Who'd have imagined?

So the first part of her plan was a success; now she just had to keep going. She had to keep finding ways to remind Enzo what was important about this place. And so far she had no plan of action for today. Worst of all, the day was almost over.

They'd just finished dinner, which they'd shared since they were the only two staying at the estate. They'd agreed that in order to make it fair, one would cook and the other would clean up—though they both always seemed to share cleanup duty.

Tonight Sylvie was washing the pans, and Enzo was drying, when the front door chimed. They both turned to each other with a puzzled look on their faces.

Sylvie was the first to speak. "I'm not expecting anyone."

"Neither am I." Enzo set aside the pan and towel.

As he headed for the door, Sylvie dried off her hands. They didn't get a lot of visitors at the estate now that the hotel was closed. Curiosity got the best of her and she turned for the front door.

She rushed to catch up with Enzo. But with

his long legs and swift strides, she didn't have a chance to catch him before he reached the door. So she hung back. After all, this wasn't her home—not really. And soon she'd have to move—whether she wanted to or not.

She stood in the hallway as Enzo swung the door open. What—ahem, or should she say who—stood there was surprising, to say the least. A clown.

Like a real clown with curly, fire engine-red hair that poked out in all directions and a little black boiler hat on top. In his hand was a fistful of red ribbons leading to at least two dozen helium balloons. His face was painted white with his eyes outlined in black. And red paint had his mouth painted into a permanent smile.

When Sylvie realized her mouth was gaping she pushed her lips together, but they immediately bowed up into a smile as laughter bubbled up inside her. What in the world?

The clown wore a red jumper of sorts with a big lace collar.

Before Enzo could speak, because obviously he was having problems making sense of what he was seeing, the clown broke out into a rendition of the birthday song topped off with a little dance. Sylvie couldn't hold back her amusement. This was just too much.

Apparently, her laughter came out louder than she'd hoped because Enzo turned to her and frowned. His grumpy scowl just made her laugh that much harder. Whoever did this had definitely caught him off guard. And then she realized who would have done this. His sisters.

Sylvie reached for her phone in her pocket and started recording. The clown danced around, sang and then bowed at the end.

Enzo didn't say a word. The clown looked at him expectantly. Enzo stood as though he'd turned to stone. He really needed to lighten up.

Hoping to defuse the situation, Sylvie rushed forward to stand next to Enzo. She applauded the clown, who handed over the balloons to Enzo.

"Wait," the clown said, "there's one more thing."

The clown rushed back to his car. Yes, it was a little clown car with a black top hat, different-colored spots all over it and a big red nose on the hood. It was quite… She couldn't find the right word, so she settled for *unusual*. Sylvie wasn't even sure how the man fit in the car.

"Did you do this?" Enzo's voice rumbled with unhappiness.

"Oh, no." She held up her hands as she shook her head. But the smile just wouldn't fade from her face. This was priceless. "I had absolutely nothing to do with it. I'm innocent. I swear."

As soon as he absorbed what she'd told him, she saw the flicker of light go on in his eyes. "My sisters. They did this."

"That would be my guess."

His scowl darkened. "Wait until I see them again."

"You'll what?" She knew it was an empty threat. He loved his sisters dearly.

She'd always longed to be a part of a bigger family. She wanted at least a sister. Someone to style hair with and paint their nails. It would have been amazing to have someone to grow up with—to share the good and the bad.

Instead, it was just her and her mother. Thank goodness they had good friends and neighbors. But it wasn't quite the same as having brothers and sisters of her own—not to mention a father. A pang of sorrow settled in her chest.

And now, after observing Enzo and his sisters, she couldn't help but envy their closeness, the way they teased each other and the way they pulled together. It was special. And sometimes she wondered if Enzo realized just how special a relationship he had with his sisters. Sylvie would give anything to have just a little part of that family camaraderie.

Before Enzo could answer, the clown returned with a white box. "This is for you. I hope you have a happy birthday."

"It's not my birthday," Enzo said grumpily.

The clown's forehead scrunched up. He shrugged, turned and walked away.

Enzo closed the door. "When my sisters said they had something special planned, I had no idea they'd go this far."

Sylvie lightly elbowed him. "Lighten up. They just wanted to make you smile. Not scowl like you're doing now."

"I'm not scowling." His brows were still drawn together as his lips pressed into a firm line.

"Really?" She arched a brow at him as she smiled.

"I'm not." He attempted a smile but it didn't work out. The disgruntled look on his face only succeeded in sending her into another fit of giggles. Immediately, his frown returned.

It took her a moment or two to gather herself. "So what's in the box?"

He glanced down at the white box in his hand as though he'd totally forgotten. He let go of all the balloons when he went to open the box. Both of their heads lifted as the balloons sailed up and up in the two-story foyer.

"Great." Enzo frowned at them. "Now, how am I supposed to get those down?"

"You aren't. They'll come down in time." She studied him as he stared up at the balloons. "You did get helium balloons as a kid, didn't you?"

He shook his head. "No balloons. Just a nice dinner, cake and a couple of presents."

Sylvie couldn't believe she had something over on him. Her mother had planned themed birthday parties with balloons and hats and whatever else she could think of. Enzo might have had the big, loving family that she'd always wanted, but her mother had doted on her and given her other special memories that she hadn't thought of in a very long time.

"What?" Enzo was studying her.

"Um, nothing. I was just remembering my birthdays from when I was a kid."

"What were they like?"

She shrugged. "My mother would invite all of the local kids and she'd always have a theme. One year it was jungle animals. She would have games and little prizes. Nothing that cost much but just enough to make the kids feel special."

"Those sound like some good memories."

"They are. And thank you for helping me to remember." But she didn't want to dwell on the past and all that she'd lost since then. "So what's in the box?"

She moved over next to him as he lifted the lid. They both peered inside to find a beautiful cake. The background was white frosting but the decorations were deep purple flowers, hunter green leaves and a gold vine winding its way around the cake as though it was some sort of wreath.

She couldn't help but think of the vineyard when she looked at the cake. Sylvia wondered if his sisters had picked the decorations out intentionally. Of course, there weren't any grapes or barrels, but the color scheme with the purple flowers and green leaves on a vine certainly resembled the vineyard. She couldn't help but wonder if Bianca and Gia were sending their brother a message. Were they gently urging him to keep the estate?

Sylvie's gaze moved to Enzo. His scowl had softened. In fact, there was a small smile pulling at the corners of his lips. He liked the cake? And the reminder of the vineyard that he was selling?

She glanced back at the cake and then realized she'd missed the rest of the decoration. In the center of the cake in purple frosting was scrolled out *To The Best Brother.*

"Aww..." Sylvie smiled. "That's so sweet."

"But so not true." He closed the box.

"Of course it is."

He shook his head. "If it was, I wouldn't have let them down when they needed me most."

He walked away before she could respond. Not that she knew what to say to that. Enzo was being harder on himself than he should be. Sure, he was selling the estate, but that didn't make him a bad brother. She had to help him see this if she had any hope of him changing his mind about selling the estate.

* * *

Why was everyone making such a fuss?

Enzo placed the cake box on the kitchen counter. His sisters knew he didn't like a fuss being made over his birthday. A card was fine. It was discreet but meaningful. What his sisters had done was big, loud and embarrassing. They did it because they felt guilty over forgetting his birthday.

Honestly, he couldn't blame them. They had new, exciting lives now. He would, too. As soon as he concluded the sale of the estate. Which meant he had to talk to Sylvie about the weddings she had scheduled. They'd either have to hold off the sale or, preferably, move the events to another location. He'd even pick up the tab for moving them elsewhere.

"Do you mind if I cut the cake?" Sylvie's voice interrupted his thoughts.

His gaze moved from her to the cake and back again. "You want to eat it?"

Her fine brows drew together. "That is the purpose of cake, isn't it?"

"Uh, yes. Go ahead." He was flustered and not making sense.

The truth was that he was dreading their upcoming conversation. He knew how much the wedding business meant to Sylvie. That was why he'd let her continue the business after he'd shut down the hotel. But now he had a potential buyer and he couldn't put the conversation off any longer.

Maybe talking over cake would make what he said easier to take. Oh, who was he kidding? This wasn't going to be easy.

He thought after he told her he was selling the estate that she would have been angry with him, but instead, she'd thrown him a birthday party. What was up with that?

Maybe it was shock. Maybe the reality wasn't sinking in. Or maybe she'd misunderstood him and thought he said he was thinking about selling.

This evening he had to make sure she understood this sale was a certainty. And they needed to figure out dates for winding up the wedding business. He was pretty certain from what the buyer had said that he wouldn't be inclined to open up any part of the estate for strangers to come in, either to tour the winery or to host a wedding.

And for that, Enzo felt awful. He didn't want

to hurt Sylvie. She'd been nothing but kind to him. But he would make this up to her. He wasn't sure how yet, but he'd figure out a way.

"I thought we'd eat dessert outside. It's such a lovely and warm evening." Sylvie held a plate with a slice of chocolate cake out to him.

He accepted her offer and followed her to the veranda. It was one of his favorite parts of the house. The veranda was spacious and yet it wasn't too big. It overlooked the vines and that normally made him smile. There was just something about the fresh earth, the abundant vines and the promise of a bountiful harvest that made him happy.

But right now his attention was fully focused on Sylvie. She moved toward the balustrade and then turned back to him. With the setting sun splashing brilliant oranges, pinks and purples across the sky, it was like she'd just stepped into a painting. And he was totally captivated by her beauty, both inside and out.

For a moment he imagined what it might be like if they'd carried on their fling after returning from Paris. Would they have romantic evenings like this followed by passionate, sleepless nights?

Or would their hot flame have burnt out by now? If so, where would that have left them? He definitely didn't think they'd be standing here sharing cake.

He told himself he was right to end things when he did. But looking at Sylvie now with her hair down over her shoulders and a light breeze combing through her silky hair, he didn't feel right. He felt like he'd made the biggest mistake of his life.

"Aren't you going to sit down?" Her voice jarred him from his thoughts.

"No. I have to check a new valve we installed at the winery earlier today. And if I sit down now, I might not move again."

"I understand. I have days like that."

They turned back to the beautiful scenery. They ate their cake in silence. The cake was so delicate that it practically melted on his tongue. The mascarpone frosting was whipped to perfection. And the berry filling gave the cake a pop of flavor. He might have preferred skipping the singing clown but his sisters had outdone themselves with this cake.

All too soon the cake was gone. And the moment he'd been dreading had arrived. How did he say this to her without ruining this easiness that they'd regained? Maybe that was it. Maybe he should let her know how much all of this meant to him.

"I should get moving," she said. "I need to go over my to-do list for the wedding this weekend." She took his empty plate from him, stacking it with her own and then turned toward the house.

"Wait," he said, still trying to figure out how to word this.

She turned back to him with curiosity showing in her eyes. "What do you need?"

"I need to talk to you." He rubbed his damp palms down over his jeans. "I mean, I wanted to apologize to you about Paris."

"We've been over this. I really don't want to talk about it."

"I know. I'm sorry. What I was trying to tell you in my own jumbled way is that I don't want it to ruin our friendship."

"It hasn't." She sent him a reassuring smile. "You and I, we'll always be friends."

He stepped toward her. His gaze met hers. "Do you really mean that?"

"I do." There had been no hesitation in her words.

"Thank you."

"For what?"

"Giving me a second chance."

She had no idea how much her words meant to him. It wasn't until that moment that he realized just how important their relationship was to him. She meant more to him than he was willing to admit, even to himself.

His gaze dipped to her lips. There was a tiny dab of frosting on her bottom lip. He longed to lean forward and lick it off her berry-red lips. The urge swelled within him.

The truth was that he couldn't forget about their steamy encounter in Paris. It haunted his dreams at night. Teasing and taunting him.

During the day he thought he'd finally gotten a handle on things. But standing here so close to Sylvie, he realized that he'd only been fooling himself. She had gotten into his blood and he had no idea how to undo the spell she had over him.

When he lifted his gaze upward, he noticed the twinkle of interest in her eyes. Desire stirred in his gut. In that moment he started to question his judgment. Maybe just a little kiss wouldn't be so bad. After all, she didn't seem to reject the idea. In fact, the look in her beautiful brown eyes was one of interest. She was interested in him?

Was it possible she didn't regret their night together like he'd been imagining? Had he jumped to all the wrong conclusions?

He halted his rambling thoughts. He stepped back and raked his fingers through his hair. He couldn't believe he'd almost talked himself into kissing her.

"Sorry about that," he said. "I need to get going."

Before she could say anything, he strode away. He didn't trust himself to stay there in the last lingering rays of the sun with the most beautiful woman he'd ever known.

It wasn't until he was almost to the vineyard that he realized he hadn't done what he'd set out to do. He hadn't talked to her about winding down the wedding business. And now he was hesitant to go near her again. She had to know that he'd almost kissed her.

His feet kept moving. Their talk could wait

for another day—a day when he had his head screwed on straight.

Sylvie was off-limits to him. It was the way it had to be. He refused to hurt her again when he couldn't commit to a relationship—not when he let down the people closest to him.

CHAPTER SIX

HAD THAT REALLY HAPPENED?

Had Enzo almost kissed her?

Saturday morning Sylvie was still thinking about that moment on the veranda a few nights ago. In fact, it'd taken up a lot of her thoughts. Perhaps too many because she'd had to rush to put the finishing touches on this wedding. A wedding that was about to take place in the garden.

And yet, when she was supposed to be checking last-minute things off on her to-do list, she was thinking about the way Enzo had stared into her eyes—the desire that had flashed in them. And then there was the way his look had sent her heart racing.

At times his gaze could be so intent that it was like he could see straight through her—like he could see what made her tick. All this time she'd been fooling herself into thinking she had kept her attraction to him under wraps—that there was no way he knew just how much she wished he would pull her into his arms and kiss her. But then what?

This is where things got really muddled. In her daydreams and for that matter, in her nighttime dreams, she never got past the arms wrapped around each other and the lips pressing to each other. She supposed it was because she couldn't imagine what normally came next—a loving and committed relationship.

The truth was relationships didn't last. She'd learned that lesson over and over again in her life. It was best to just keep things light and simple.

Because putting her tattered heart on the line wasn't something she was willing to do. The thought of letting herself feel deeply for Enzo and then losing him—she gave herself a mental shake. It wasn't going to happen. She wouldn't let it.

The only reason she had planned the surprise party was to remind Enzo of what he had here at the estate—what he would lose if he were to sell it. The party, the cake and all the other arrangements she'd seen to… Well, those had nothing to do with her feelings for him because…because she had those all under control.

So how did she explain what had happened in Paris? It was that city—the city of love. It had cast some sort of spell over her—over them. But once they'd returned to Tuscany, they were both able to see what a mistake they'd made. There was nothing between them—nothing more than a casual friendship.

Okay, maybe that wasn't quite true. Maybe it was more like a close friendship—at least that was the way things used to be. Enzo used to confide in her and she had done the same with him. But ever since that one night, there had been an awkwardness between them—much like a wall. One that each of them had taken some comfort in hiding behind. But now it was getting in her way. Now she needed to knock it down, if she was going to convince him not to sell the estate.

Ring. Ring.

It was the house phone. The only thing it was used for these days was business. Personal calls went to their cell phones. Sylvie checked the time on her fitness tracker. There was less than an hour now until the wedding ceremony. Surely, this wasn't bad news regarding the wedding.

The phone rang again.

Her gaze quickly skimmed down over her checklist. No. Everything was done and the caterer had already set up finger food in the dining room. There was nothing to worry about.

And yet, as she picked up the phone, she couldn't help but wonder if this phone call would somehow help or hinder her efforts to keep her home and a job at which she was quite skilled.

"Hello. This is the Barto Vineyard. How may I help you?"

"Hello. My name is Jameson Asaro and I'm with *Tuscany Views* magazine. We're interested in doing a big spread about your vineyard and the prestigious award your winery won in Paris."

"Oh. Wow." Her mind was racing. This could be the help she needed to sway Enzo's decision about keeping or selling the estate. "That would be wonderful."

"Can I take that as confirmation that you'd like us to visit the estate to do our research for the article?"

"Um, can you hold on for a moment?"

"Sure."

She pushed a button on the phone, putting it on hold while she fished her cell phone out of her pocket. She quick-dialed Enzo. The phone rang and rang before going to voice mail.

She knew if Enzo was out in the fields that there were many places with no reception. Of all the days for him to be out of reach. Frustration balled up in her stomach. This was so important.

She moved the landline receiver back to her ear. "I'm sorry about that. I was just trying to reach someone at the vineyard. Could we get back to you—?"

"I don't think you understand the urgency of this. We just had a last-minute cancellation and we need a big story. Something we can cover right away."

"Oh. I… I…uh…" What was she supposed to say? She tried to imagine Enzo's response. Would he welcome the coverage? It was really special. This online and print magazine stretched throughout Italy and beyond its borders. It was quite a coup.

"I need a decision now." The man's voice was firm.

Her palms grew damp. The last thing she wanted to do was to make the wrong decision and have Enzo upset with her. As it was, they were just starting to find an easiness with each other after Paris. If she were to make the wrong choice here and they went back to acting like strangers again, she'd never convince him that selling the estate was a big mistake—a huge mistake.

But what if she were to pass on the publicity, would Enzo get upset? In fact, she'd been so busy worrying about what he'd do if she were to accept the offer that she hadn't stopped to think about it in reverse. Turning down the offer could be a mistake, too. Either way it was a gamble.

Her stomach knotted knowing the man on the other end of the phone was expecting her to make a decision now—right now. And if she picked the wrong one, it could mean losing her ability to reason with Enzo.

She worried her bottom lip. All her attention was focused on whether she should or shouldn't. Should or shouldn't. The words revolved around in her mind at a dizzying pace—

"Hello," the man said, "are you still there?"

The moment of truth had arrived. "Um, yes, I am."

"And are you willing to do the article?"

"Yes." The word popped out of her mouth and then she realized it was too late to take it back. Her fate had been sealed. She just didn't know how any of this was going to work out. And dealing with the unknown was something she didn't do well. She liked plans and certainties.

"Very good. We'll arrive Thursday."

"As in this coming Thursday? Less than a week from now?"

"Yes, ma'am. Is that a problem?"

A problem? Not that she could think of, but Enzo might have a differing opinion. "No, it's not."

"Good. We'll need a tour of the vineyard. We're going to need photos."

"Photos?" She hadn't considered what all would be involved with this.

"Yes, we'll need photos to go along with the write-up."

"Of course." She would normally have anticipated this if her thoughts weren't being pulled in so many different directions.

Thankfully, the estate was in tip-top shape. So pictures shouldn't be a big deal. Right? Surely, Enzo would be happy about this interest in the vineyard, wouldn't he?

She assured herself that she had nothing to worry about. After concluding the phone call, she wrote Enzo a note and left it in what was now his office. And then she set off to change into her dress for the wedding. It was almost time for the bride and groom to say *I do.*

What was wrong with him?

Every time Enzo was in Sylvie's vicinity, he was nearly kissing her or thinking about kissing her. And that just wasn't right. He was the one taking away not only her job but also her home.

And there was another thing. He kept delaying talking to her about the final date for the last wedding at the estate. No matter how much he dreaded doing it, the talk had to take place. In fact, he'd put it off too long as it was.

After a long day in the fields, he had one

more thing he needed to do. He wanted to test these new oak barrels for leakage and then he would head to the little guesthouse on the property where Sylvie lived. He was certain she wouldn't want to see him, not after the way he'd handled himself earlier that week—or rather how he'd been out of control, letting his desire dictate his actions. That was why he'd been up extra early every morning and returned late each evening.

"Something on your mind?" Vito asked.

"No. Why?"

Vito nodded toward the hose. "Because you're spilling water all over the floor."

"What?" Enzo glanced down to see that the barrel was full and the excess water was forming a puddle on the floor. He rushed to turn off the water. When the hose was drained, he turned to an amused Vito. "Aren't you supposed to be on holiday with your family?"

"I just stopped on my way out of town to check on things and see if you need anything."

Enzo grabbed a rag to clean up his mess. This accident was minor but it was indicative of why he didn't belong here any longer. He was forever distracted. Where once his work had been all-encompassing and fulfilling, now his mind was on other things. "Thanks, but I don't need a thing. Have a good trip."

Vito didn't say a word for a moment. He just stared thoughtfully at him.

Enzo grew uncomfortable beneath his friend's stare. "Whatever it is, just say it."

"I'm wondering what's on your mind." Vito's expression turned serious. "Or should I say *who*?"

Enzo shook his head. "No one is on my mind." *Liar.* "I just have a lot to do before the estate sale goes through."

For a moment a strained silence filled the air. Enzo knew Vito didn't agree with his decision to sell the estate. They'd already had a heated disagreement. Enzo was hoping Vito would accept the inevitable, even if he didn't agree with him. Enzo was certain the new owner would keep him on to manage the place, as they'd already discussed it.

"Seems like Sylvie is trying to sway you into changing your mind about the sale," Vito said as he propped himself up against the worktable.

Enzo moved around the barrel, searching for

any leaks. So far it looked good. "She's wasting her time. It's practically a done deal."

"You didn't sign the papers, did you?" There was concern in Vito's voice.

"No. But I will as soon as we work out the final terms."

"So there's still time for you to change your mind?"

"It's not going to happen." If this was anyone but his father's best friend, he would have told Vito to buzz off already. But Vito was a part of the family. He was like his uncle and no matter how much he stepped on Enzo's nerves, he just couldn't tell him to get lost.

"Did you ever consider raising your family here? Maybe with Sylvie."

That was it. He wasn't getting away with that—favorite uncle or not. Enzo straightened to his full height. But when he turned, he found Vito had already made a hasty exit. No one could ever accuse Vito of not being a wise man because right about now Enzo was about to unload all of his pent-up frustration when—

"Enzo?" It was Sylvie's voice. "Enzo, are you in here?"

"Back here," he called out. It was only after

he'd spoken that he realized the mistake he'd made. He was in no frame of mind to deal with her. He was certain she'd want to talk about that almost-kiss and want to analyze its meaning.

Her footsteps approached and he braced himself for her anger or accusations. He just needed to get it over quickly and then he'd tell her that he needed her final date for the wedding business. Quick. Simple.

He gave himself a mental shake. Nothing was simple when it came to Sylvie. It was more like complicated and confusing. But Vito had been right. She was doing everything in her power to sway his decision about the sale. It wasn't going to work. But that didn't keep him from wondering what she'd try next.

"Oh, there you are." She joined him at the worktable.

"What did you need?"

"Did you happen to see the note I left you in the office?"

He shook his head. "I haven't been in the house since this morning. I always make plans to stay far away on wedding days."

"I don't blame you." It was the first time she'd said something like that.

"You make it sound like you don't like the weddings."

She shrugged. "I just know they get loud and congested. And if you don't have to be there, it's best to find a nice quiet corner of the estate. I know that's what I'd do if I could."

He wasn't sure what she was trying to tell him. And he wasn't in the mood to figure it out. But since she was here and before he forgot, he said, "Sylvie, we have to talk about the wedding business."

When her gaze met his, there was a sadness in her eyes. The look tore at his gut. It felt like no matter what decision he made it was going to be the wrong answer for someone.

But Sylvie was smart and talented. She would land on her feet. And it wasn't like he was planning to kick her to the curb. He would pay for her moving costs and her housing until she was able to get settled. He'd even help her find another job, not that he knew anything about weddings. Still, he would do what he could with job references and utilizing all of his contacts.

“What about it?” she asked in a softer voice than normal.

He sighed. This was so much harder than he’d imagined. “We need to set a final close date for the business.” When she didn’t say anything but instead stood there looking at him like he was the enemy, he said, “I’m sorry things worked out like this.”

He didn’t know what he expected—for her to yell at him or to stomp off. But she did neither of those things. She started naming off weddings from memory. They were weddings that stretched well into the next year. He knew canceling them would create a lot of drama for not only Sylvie but also the couples and their families. The guilt mounted.

“When you told me the estate was to be sold,” Sylvie said, “I started working out a plan. I spoke with a stellar wedding planner in Florence. She was willing to take on some of my clients. And the ones she couldn’t fit into her schedule, I plan to handle myself but with a different venue. I just have one final wedding here at the estate.”

“You did all of this already?”

She looked at him like, *well, of course*. “I

couldn't afford to wait around and hope something would change. We're talking about the biggest day in someone's life. I couldn't ruin it and so I've been spending most of my time making alternative plans."

"I bet it didn't go well."

She glanced away and shook her head. "There were a lot of upset people."

"I'm sorry, Sylvie. I never meant to put you in such an awful position." Once again he hadn't been able to spare the feelings of someone he cared about. If only he'd thought of all the ramifications of selling the estate; maybe he could have made this easier on Sylvie. He wasn't sure how and it really didn't matter now. The damage was done. "What did you come here to tell me?"

She wrung her hands together. "There was an important phone call this morning, while you were out in the fields. I tried to reach you."

His gut twisted up in a knot of worry. "Was it my sisters? Did something happen to one of them?"

"No." She shook her head. "Sorry. I didn't mean to worry you. It's nothing like that."

He blew out a pent-up breath. “Then what was this important call?”

“It was about your big win in Paris.” She sent him a smile that didn’t quite reach her eyes. “Word is out and *Tuscany Views* magazine wants your story.”

“My story?” He shook his head. “I don’t have a story. You told them to go away, didn’t you?” When she didn’t immediately answer, a feeling of dread came over him. “Sylvie, what did you do?”

“All they want is to speak with you and take some photos.”

“Impossible.”

“Why? You deserve this. You work hard around this vineyard.”

“Because…” His mind raced for a reason the interview and article were a bad idea, aside from the fact that he didn’t feel he was deserving. “Because this place isn’t set up for photos.”

“What? Of course it is. It’s always kept up for vineyard tours and wine-tasting parties.”

“Not anymore. I’ve started taking things down and packing up the place for the new owner.”

It was then that she glanced around at the

bare walls. She moved to the doorway of the large wine-tasting room. There was nothing left on the walls or shelves. The room was bare except for the furniture because he had yet to find someone willing to buy it.

All the vineyard's rich history was now boxed up and put in storage. He didn't know what to do with it all. He was going to talk to his sisters about the wall hangings and plaques as well as the photos. It was a lot to go through.

"It shouldn't take long to put it all back up," Sylvie said with a hopeful note in her voice.

"When is this reporter supposed to be here?"

"Thursday."

"As in five days from now?"

Sylvie nodded. "See. Plenty of time."

At last, he had his out without hurting her feelings. "Not enough time with just one person to do it all and look after the vineyard."

"One person?" Her fine brows drew together. "But what about Vito and the others?"

"Vito is off on holiday. So are a couple of other guys. They needed a break before harvest. And the other guys are busy clearing a new field to be planted for next season. The new owner wants to expand the vineyard."

"Oh. Okay." Sylvie paused as she processed this information. "We can still do this. I'll help you."

He shook his head. "I don't think so. It's not your job."

"But I told them you'd do it and I didn't get their number so I can't call them back."

"It's a magazine. I'm sure you can call the office and they'll put you through to the reporter."

"I didn't catch their name."

He frowned at her. He had a feeling no matter what he said she'd counter it with an answer. He knew where she was going with this. She was hoping this interview and media coverage would change his mind about selling the estate. It wouldn't.

But she was so intent on him doing this that he felt as though he owed it to her after he'd ended her wedding business. "Okay."

Her eyes widened. "Okay, what?"

"We'll do it."

"You'll do the interview and let them tour the estate?"

He didn't want to; he really didn't. Selling this estate wasn't easy for him, and reminding himself of everything he was about to turn his back on wouldn't help matters. But all the good memories were interlaced with all the bad memories—things he wanted to forget.

Still, when Sylvie looked at him with hope in her eyes, how could he turn her down? Right now he felt if she asked him for the stars and the moon, he'd climb the tallest ladder and gather them for her.

But he also remembered what Vito said about Sylvie doing anything she could to change his mind about selling the estate. He couldn't allow her to get her hopes up that he would reverse his decision and then have her crushed once more.

He cleared his throat. "Sylvie, I'll do the interview and tour, but you need to realize that I'm not going to change my mind about selling the estate. It's going to be sold."

Emotion flashed in her eyes, but in a blink it was gone before he could make it out. "I understand. Thank you for agreeing to do this. It'll make a really nice memory for you and your sisters."

He didn't know about that. Still, he kept putting one foot in front of the other as he marched toward the estate sale. He'd made the decision to turn his back on this place and it had seemed right at the time. So then why was he starting to get the feeling it was the worst decision he'd ever made?

CHAPTER SEVEN

WOULD THIS WORK?

Sylvie hoped so.

But how had Enzo figured out what she was up to? Sylvie thought she was being so stealthy, and all along he knew she was trying to sway his decision about selling the estate. So much for her secretiveness.

But maybe this was better. He knew where she stood on the sale. Why keep it a secret? If someone vocalized their opposition to the sale, perhaps he'd rethink his decision. Not that her opinion was that important to him or anything. Still, he might listen to her, if she could do it the right way.

It wasn't until he mentioned he had been packing things that she realized there were photos and mementos missing from the main house. Now she knew where they'd gone. Enzo was slowly and steadily removing signs of the Bartolini family from the estate—like some sort of human eraser. She had to wonder if by removing the physical things if it would remove whatever memories were attached to them. Was it really that easy to turn your back on the past?

It was midmorning by the time Sylvie made it to the winery. She'd intended to be there much earlier, but she'd gotten caught up finding a new venue for an upcoming wedding. It broke her heart to turn away business, but Enzo wasn't giving her much option.

When she stepped into the winery, she found Enzo making notes on his digital tablet. "Sorry I'm late. I had some work that needed doing."

"If you don't have time for this we could cancel—"

"No." She shook her head. "I can manage everything." She glanced around at the bare walls. They were like canvases just waiting to be adorned with color. "I like it here."

"You do?"

She nodded. "I don't know why. Maybe because it's so different from the main house. Whereas the house is cozy and warm, this room is huge—" she gazed up at the two-story ceilings "—and it has an industrial feel with the metallic tanks. I don't know. I just like it."

Enzo glanced around as if trying to see it the way she did. "I spent a lot of time down here as a kid. This was the best room to hide in when playing hide-and-seek with my sisters. They were afraid of the big tanks so they didn't venture in here much."

She smiled as she imagined Enzo as a small child. "So what you're saying is that you cheated."

"I did not. I won fair and square. They could have come in here, if they'd wanted."

"Uh-huh." She continued to smile as she shook her head. "And your father didn't mind you playing in here."

"He minded. But he didn't know everything that went on."

"So you were sneaky, too?"

His dark brows drew together. "Hey. I don't think I like the picture you're painting of me as a child."

"Just calling it like I see it." She laughed at his look of outrage.

"I definitely don't want you talking to the reporter." He turned, setting the tablet on the worktable. He retrieved a utility knife and moved off to the side of the table where there was a stack of cardboard boxes. He sliced open the tape on the top of one.

"I could give them a more balanced story," she said, enjoying this bit of banter. It'd been far too long since they'd had this much fun together. This day was definitely looking up. "With what I'm learning about you, they could do an exposé about the real man behind the image."

His brows drew together. "What image?"

"Oh, I don't know. The handsome winemaker with an award-winning touch."

His frown lines smoothed as a smile lifted the corners of his mouth. "I wouldn't give up your wedding work. Journalism definitely isn't your calling."

"What? I liked that tag line. Maybe this is better—Sexy Winemaker Wins Big."

"First, who is this sexy person? And second, it wasn't that big."

"And who's being modest now?"

He didn't answer her as he lined up the framed prints on the table. "These are the photos we had hung in here for the tours that give a brief tutorial of the winemaking process."

She moved next to him. She gazed down at the photos that she'd seen numerous times in the past, but this time she saw them differently. Instead of telling the story of how grapes were turned into wine, she saw the story of Enzo's past.

In the first photo was a picture of a woman picking grapes. She was smiling brightly while holding a cluster of grapes. Sylvie didn't need to be told; it was clear it was his mother. Carla Bartolini had been a beautiful woman, just like her daughters.

Sylvie made her way down the table, looking at each photo. Enzo quietly followed her. She wanted to ask him what he was thinking but she didn't want to disturb the moment.

She paused in front of the photo of a man in this very room. Though she'd never met Aldo Bartolini, she knew without a doubt it was Enzo's father. The resemblance was that great.

There were other photos of Enzo and his sisters when they were young. In one framed photo, the entire family was standing in front of four large holding tanks. "You all look so happy."

"Looks can be deceiving," he muttered.

"Really?" Her gaze moved from him to the photo and back to him again. "Are you saying you and your family weren't happy in this photo?"

"I'm saying I don't know." He moved next to her and stared at the photo. "I thought we were happy. But now I know all those happy moments were covering up big secrets. I don't know what was real and what was just for show."

"Maybe you don't need to figure it out. Maybe you just need to accept the memories the way they are in your mind. I'm sure your parents would want that for you."

"But how can they be so happy when they were keeping something so explosive from us?"

"Perhaps it's because they'd made peace with their decision. They had to believe they were doing the right thing for their family. And then they let it go because otherwise it would have destroyed the family you knew. Just like you need to let go of the anger at them and the guilt you've heaped on yourself before it destroys you."

He shook his head. "I don't know if I can do that. You don't understand."

Sylvie turned to him. "Why are you so willing to just reject the happiness you felt? It was a real and genuine emotion. You should be embracing it instead of rejecting it."

"Is that what you're doing? Embracing the good memories of your mother?"

"I'm trying."

"But you're still blaming yourself for not being there for her as much as you feel you should have been."

She nodded.

"Then how is that so different from what I'm doing?"

She glanced away. She supposed that in a way, it wasn't. Maybe they both had some letting-go to do. Maybe it was what they both needed to do before either of them could be truly happy.

And then she remembered something she'd forgotten in her grief. It was a conversation with her mother near the end. Sylvie had been apologizing for having to leave for work when her mother had told her she understood. And she was proud of her. She said that Sylvie was the best daughter she could have ever hoped for. And that soon she would be reunited with Sylvie's father, and both of them would be watching over her, smiling down upon her. She urged Sylvie to find a love like that for herself—a love that would last all of eternity.

Sylvie's gaze moved to Enzo. What would her mother make of him? Would she tell Sylvie to cut her losses and leave the estate? She had so many questions. In this moment she missed her mother with such a fierce intensity.

"Sylvie, are you okay?" The concern in Enzo's voice drew her from her thoughts.

She glanced at him. "What?"

"You're crying."

"I am?" She ran her fingers over her cheeks. They were damp. "I'm sorry. I was just remembering a conversation with my mother."

"It must have been serious."

"It was one of the times when I had to leave her to go to work and she told me she understood. She said she was proud of me. I can't believe I'd forgotten that." She left out the part about finding true love. She didn't want Enzo reading anything into it. Her gaze met his. "Thank you."

"For what? Making you cry?"

"No." She smiled. "For giving me back a memory—an important memory."

"You're welcome, though I don't think I did anything."

"Sometimes it's just having someone to listen. And you were that someone today."

He smiled at her. "Let's put these prints back on the wall."

"Sounds like a plan." They set to work side by side.

Enzo honestly didn't think he'd said much of anything important.

But Sylvie seemed to think differently.

For the next few days they worked together as a team cleaning, sorting and arranging. Sylvie had been extra nice to him. If he had sparked a memory in her mind, he was happy he'd been able to do that for her.

Trying to remember the past wasn't his problem. He clearly recalled his past with his parents and the illusion of a happy family. The problem was he also remembered the carnage and agony after both of his parents died.

That stupid journal had compounded matters. Why had his mother kept it? If they hadn't read it, no one would have been the wiser. Well, that wasn't true. He knew the secret. At least some of it. And the guilt for keeping that information to himself was something that dogged his steps throughout the estate.

They'd hung the prints in the tank room. And then they'd moved to the main house, putting family photos back on the walls—some of his immediate family and others of their ancestors in black-and-white photos. By the time they had the villa fully decorated, Monday was over and they were exhausted.

Come Tuesday morning, they put back all the decorations in the barrel and tank room in the winery. There was only one room left. The wine-tasting room was part museum and part tasting space for visitors. It had taken Enzo days to take everything down and pack it away.

He glanced around at the bare, expansive walls that used to hold a collage of vineyard history. "I don't know if we're going to get this all done."

"Sure we are." Sylvie's gaze followed his before returning to him. She sent him a reassuring smile. "We just have to hurry. We'll put everything back where it came from. It will save us the time of having to figure out where things should go."

He didn't see where that would save much time. But there was no time to argue. So while he moved the squared black display stands with glass tops back into position, Sylvie opened one storage box after the next, unwrapping awards, novelties and plaques with descriptions of each item. Enzo wasn't sure why he'd packed absolutely everything but every time he went to part with something, he found a reason not to do so. His sisters might want it. The item might be valuable. Vito might want some of it. There was always an excuse close at hand.

"I have some photos on my phone that might help us put the smaller things back where they were." Sylvie pulled out her phone and placed it on the table.

Curiosity had him walking over and taking a look. There were a number of photos, not only of the wine-tasting room but also of the main house and the surrounding grounds. "Are you an amateur photographer?"

"Hardly. I just love this place and I wanted to be able to remember it. You don't mind, do you?"

"No. Not at all."

"I bet the young, ambitious you in these photos would have never imagined this day would come."

As Enzo gazed at the old family photos, he heard his father's voice in his mind: *Life never goes the way you plan. It's finding your way through life's detours that's worth the effort.*

Enzo realized this was his detour in life. He just had no idea where it was going to lead him. First, he had to wind things up here at the estate and it was proving to be more complicated than he'd ever imagined.

"Enzo?" Sylvie was giving him a strange look. "Everything okay?"

"Um, yeah. Fine. Let's get these things where they belong."

And so they worked for a while in silence. He couldn't believe she'd talked him into putting all of this stuff back. What was it about Sylvie that he was willing to do things he wouldn't do otherwise?

"What do you think?" Sylvie's gaze moved around the room. "Think we'll get it done today?"

"Today? Do you have something you want to do tomorrow?"

She smiled and nodded. He knew that smile. She looked that way when she had a plan he wasn't going to like, not like at all.

He pressed his hands to his waist. "Sylvie, what do you have in mind?"

"I thought we could head into Florence. I was thinking some flower arrangements and candles and maybe a wreath or two…or three would brighten up this place. The photos are a nice touch but the decor needs softening a bit."

He rubbed the back of his neck. "Don't set your heart on it."

She turned a serious gaze on him. "I'm not giving up on this. I'll go to Florence alone if I must."

Her words brought forth another memory. Enzo recalled his father standing in this very room saying to him, *Never give up on those you love.*

And another of his father's sayings: *Forgiveness is one of the greatest things you can give yourself and others.*

It was almost like his father knew this day was coming and in his cryptic way, he was guiding his son. But Enzo just couldn't brush aside what his parents' secret had done to his sisters. It wasn't right. Maybe his father should have taken some of his own advice.

"Enzo—" Sylvie's voice put a halt to his thoughts "—if you don't want to go, you can just say so. You don't have to scowl at me."

He was scowling? He hadn't realized his thoughts had transformed onto his face. With concerted effort, he smoothed the frown lines. "Sorry. It wasn't you. I just had a memory."

"Of your parents?"

He nodded. "It was of my father. He used to share with me these little bits of wisdom."

"Like what?"

Enzo told her what he could remember. As he was talking about his parents, he started to see them in a new light. They were more than a married couple running this estate with nary a hiccup. When you scratched beneath the surface, they were flawed individuals. But when you went even deeper, they were loving parents.

"Maybe you should reconsider selling the estate," she said.

He shook his head.

"But you have good memories. Maybe not all of them are happy—"

"Sylvie, stop!" He paused as though reining in his frustration. "It's too late."

"But you haven't signed any papers yet—"

"I gave my word."

"That's not the same as signing a sales agreement."

"For me it is." And with that he walked away.

Sylvie let go of the subject—for now. Instead, she focused on the work. Sooner or later she was going to have to admit defeat. Just not today.

CHAPTER EIGHT

THEY WORKED WELL TOGETHER, complementing each other's skills. He did the heavy lifting. She did the final touches.

After Enzo placed the last print on the wall, he glanced around the room. His gaze settled on Sylvie as she arranged some mementos in one of the lighted glass cases. The winery looked as it had before. No. Sylvie's little adjustment here and there had made it look picture perfect.

It was late in the evening when Enzo said, "That's it for tonight."

He noticed that Sylvie didn't argue.

He led the way to the exit. He paused by the door and flipped off the lights in the winery. He knew he wouldn't sleep that night, not with all the thoughts darting about his mind. Still, it was no reason to keep Sylvie from getting some rest.

Darkness fell over the building as they stepped

outside. He typed the code into the security pad before turning back to Sylvie. In the moonlight she looked like an enchantress. And it'd be so easy to forget all the reasons he shouldn't hold her close and kiss her like he'd wanted to the other day.

Instead, he started to walk. To head to the main house, he would need to walk straight ahead but instead he turned down the path to the left and continued moving toward the guest-house. In silence they walked in the moonlight. His thoughts were filled with memories of another night when he'd been along with Sylvie. It had been an evening they'd thrown caution to the wind. It was a night they wouldn't repeat.

All too soon they were standing outside Sylvie's door. He turned to her. "Thank you for all your help today."

"You're welcome. But I think it should be me thanking you since this photo shoot was my idea."

"I know I wasn't thrilled with the idea in the beginning. And I'm sorry."

"And now?"

"Now..." His thoughts swept back over the day and all that had happened. "I think it was a good idea. The perfect way to say goodbye—to this place." He was quick to add the last bit because no matter what, he wasn't ready to say goodbye to her.

Having Sylvie walk out of his life would be harder than saying goodbyc to his childhood home. But he supposed he deserved it, after sitting on his family's explosive secret all those years.

"Enzo, what is it?" Sylvie's voice was soft.

He shook his head. "Nothing."

She opened the door. "Come in."

"It's too late. And with us heading into the city tomorrow, you'll want to get some rest."

"Are you sure?"

He nodded. "I'll be fine."

In the moonlight he could make out the outline of her face but he couldn't read her eyes. He'd be willing to guess that there was a look of disbelief in them. But that was okay. This was all his problem, not hers.

When she stepped inside, she flipped on the lights. He'd just turned to walk away when they were plunged back into darkness.

"What in the world?" The sound of the light switch being flipped on and off filled the air.

Enzo immediately spun around. "Let me see."

The only problem was that it was pitch-dark inside the house and when he went to step through the doorway, he bumped into Sylvie. He immediately reached out to steady her. He pulled her to him, perhaps with more urgency than was necessary because all of a sudden her body was pressed against his.

In that moment he hesitated. He didn't want to let her go and she didn't seem interested in going anywhere. The thought of kissing her came rushing back to the forefront of his mind. And here in the dark, who would know?

They would know. He would know. He didn't deserve Sylvie. She was the most kind-hearted—the most generous—the most caring woman he'd ever known. And she deserved someone better than him. She deserved someone who faced challenges no matter how great and protected the people they loved. That wasn't him.

The thought doused the burning embers within him. He swallowed hard. "I…uh… should see what the problem is."

It was with great reluctance that he moved past her. She was quiet. If she knew of the torment going on within him, she didn't say a word.

Having memorized his way through most of the buildings on the estate over the years, he made his way to the kitchen. He felt around the wall for the light switch. He flicked it on and there was once again light.

He turned back to Sylvie, who was still in the shadows. "Looks like you have a burnt-out light. Which is strange because there should be two bulbs in that light fixture."

"Well, there are." There was some hesitancy in her voice. "The one bulb burnt out the other day, but I didn't get around to changing it."

"I see. No problem. I'll have it fixed for you in no time."

"But you don't have to bother tonight. You must be tired."

"I doubt I'll sleep tonight." The words had slipped past his lips before he realized he was saying too much. Sylvie would want to know why he wasn't sleeping, and he wasn't up for revealing his past. The day of looking at old photos and taking a stroll down memory lane had been more than enough for him. And most of all, he just didn't want to disappoint Sylvie.

She thought he was a nice guy, a good guy, and he wanted to remain that in her eyes.

And so he set to work, locating the items he would need. He knew someone else could tend to this in the morning, but he wanted to take care of Sylvie, just as she was trying to care for him by showing him what he would be giving up by selling the estate. Perhaps the gestures were not on the same scale, but he was doing what was needed in the moment.

A few minutes later he had the bulbs replaced. It was time to make his exit before he lost his head once again. But when he looked around, he didn't see Sylvie anywhere.

"Sylvie, everything is done." When there was no response, he said, "Sylvie?"

"Back here."

He walked to the back of the house, where the living room had been moved to make space for the wedding business in the front rooms. He found Sylvie seated on the couch.

She patted the cushion next to her. "Come have a seat."

He checked his wristwatch. "I… I don't think so." The truth was he didn't trust himself being that close to her. "It's really late."

"But you said you wouldn't sleep tonight."

That was true. He hadn't meant to tell her but it was too late to walk it back now. "I'll be fine."

"I've made you something to help you sleep." When he still didn't move—still didn't trust his judgment in this exhausted state—she said, "Come."

There was a firmness to her voice—the same sort of tone his mother would use when she meant business. It was amazing the things his mother could get people to do without raising her voice. Sylvie had that same poise and command. Someday she'd make a good mother. Of that he was certain.

And so he took a seat next to her, leaving a respectable distance between them. He couldn't help but feel this was a mistake, but he remained seated.

Sylvie held out a red mug. "Here. Drink this."

When he reached for it, their fingers brushed. A rush of anticipation electrified his body and it had absolutely nothing to do with the drink. His gaze met hers. He felt himself once more slipping under her spell. Enzo glanced away before it was too late. He stared down at the white frothy drink, knowing that any chance he'd had at getting some sleep was now officially gone.

He swallowed hard. "What is it?"

"It's some warmed milk that my mother would make for me whenever I was worked up from a nightmare or the night before a big test." She took a sip from her own cup.

He lifted the mug. The first thing that struck him was its soft fragrance. He wasn't sure about drinking it. He eyed up Sylvie as she took another healthy sip. Not wanting to hurt her feelings, because he was quite certain at this late hour she really didn't feel like going to all this bother, he took a small sip.

He swallowed. "This isn't warmed milk. Well, it's not just milk."

She smiled and nodded. "It has some honey, vanilla and a touch of lavender. Plus a few other things. Do you like it?"

"I...ah..." His lips pursed together as he considered the answer. He didn't hate it, but he didn't love it, either. "It's so unique. I don't think I've ever had anything like it before."

"Just keep sipping it. Trust me, it'll help relax you." She frowned at him. "You can't relax when you're perched on the edge of the couch as though you're ready to spring out the door at any moment. Sit back and relax."

This most definitely wasn't a good idea, but he was already sitting in her living room at this late hour; why not just lean back? It wasn't like she was going to throw herself into his arms. Was she? The thought definitely appealed to him.

Every muscle in his body was tense as he slid back over the cushion. And even when he was fully on the couch, he couldn't lean back. He sat fully upright, staying on guard, not letting down his defenses because he knew how easy it was to forget about circumstances when Sylvie was in his vicinity.

"Do you think there's anything that will change your mind about selling the place?"

It was the first time she'd come straight out and asked him the question. The answer that rushed to the back of his throat was one she didn't want to hear. He shifted his gaze to the contents of the mug. It might not be his favorite drink but it was better than having to speak and see the disappointment in Sylvie's eyes.

He held the mug to his lips and drank; all

the while he could feel Sylvie's gaze upon him. Why couldn't she just give this up? But he knew she was waiting for an answer. The woman definitely had a lot of tenacity.

He lowered the mug. "No. I'm not going to change my mind."

"Is there anything I can say or do—?"

"No, Sylvie. This is what has to be done." The debate of keeping the estate or letting go of the ghosts of the past churned within him. "You just don't understand."

"I would, if you told me." Her voice was soft but not forceful.

The secret he'd been holding in all these years came rushing forward, teetering on the edge of his tongue. He hadn't told anyone because he was ashamed. But maybe if he wanted to let go of the ghosts, he needed to be up-front with her. If he could trust anyone, it was Sylvie.

Not giving himself time to back out of this confession, he turned to her. In her eyes he saw caring and sympathy. He wasn't worthy of either. That undid his final bit of hesitation.

"Sylvie, I know this place means a lot to you, but to me, it is filled with ghosts of the past.

Lies and secrets that I just can't live with anymore. I need to move on—to start over."

"But wasn't all of that dealt with when Bianca found your mother's journal?"

"No." That single-syllable word hung in the nighttime air with all its possible implications.

He raked his fingers through his hair. Why did she keep pushing? She wasn't going to like what she uncovered. He wasn't the upstanding guy that she thought he was.

Sylvie scooted closer on the couch. She reached out, placing her hand on his thigh. It was all he could do not to jump back. Her touch was gentle and warm as she attempted to put him at ease. But didn't she realize what he'd been trying to tell her? He didn't deserve her kindness and understanding.

He jumped to his feet. He placed his mug on the end table. "I have to go."

"Enzo, wait." She rushed over to him. "I'm sorry. I pushed and I shouldn't have done that. Please forgive me."

Frustration and guilt churned in his gut. "Stop!"

Confusion clouded her eyes. "I'm sorry. I keep saying the wrong things."

"No. Stop apologizing. You haven't done anything wrong. I have. I don't deserve your sympathy. If you knew…"

The words hung there. The sentence went unfinished because he just couldn't bring himself to finish it—to ruin the illusion she had of him.

"We won't speak of it anymore." She reached for his hand and gave it a gentle tug. "Let's sit back down. You didn't finish your milk."

While his body followed her, his mind said he was making yet another mistake. He should head for the door. And yet, he kept taking one step after the other until he was seated on the couch next to her again.

Sylvie reached for her mug and then took a sip. "You should finish drinking yours before it goes cold. It's not as good then."

He reached for his abandoned mug. The sooner he finished it, the sooner he could leave and be alone with his thoughts.

"If you don't want to head into the city tomorrow," Sylvie said, "I can go alone."

He'd given his word and he intended to keep it. "I'll be ready to go first thing in the morning."

"But you'll be tired—"

"So will you." He wanted her to quit being so nice to him because it just made him feel worse.

But if he were to tell her the truth—tell her the deep, dark secret that he'd been keeping for years, then she'd realize she didn't have to work so hard to be nice to him. In fact, she'd probably be anxious to leave the estate and start over somewhere else—just like his sisters had done after the journal had revealed the fractures in their perfect family.

"If you ever want to talk," she said, "I mean really talk, I'm a good listener."

"Sylvie, stop." He didn't look at her. He knew if he did, he'd never get the words out. "You don't understand what's going on."

"I will," she said ever so softly, "if you tell me."

"I knew."

The words popped out before he could stop them. It was the first time he'd made a vocal admission.

Sylvie's fine brows drew together. "Knew what?"

He'd told her this much, he might as well get this over with and let the pieces fall as they may. "I knew my parents' secret—that one of us was illegitimate."

"You mean from reading the journal?"

He shook his head as he stared blindly down at the milky mixture that remained in his mug. "I knew years before my sisters read the journal."

"Oh…" Her breathy response was more of a wow response.

"As you know, I'm the oldest. And when we were kids, I got to stay up a little later than my sisters. It was only a half hour but to me it was a big deal—something Bianca and Gia didn't get to do. During that time, I would read in bed." In his mind's eye, he could see that night so clearly that it was as though he were still there. "I can't remember which book I was reading but it was one of those that you keep telling yourself you'll put down and go to sleep after one more page."

Sylvie didn't say a word. She didn't move. She just sat there taking in everything he was saying. And he knew in the end she would look at him with disappointment and think he was a coward. Rightly so.

He drew in an uneven breath. "I knew it was

late. Really late. And I heard some yelling. I was surprised because my mother always made a point of not raising her voice. She said yelling wasn't necessary to get your point across. And then I heard a door slam."

He wished he'd stayed in bed—that he'd gone to sleep when he was supposed to instead of shining a flashlight on his book and reading under the covers, because then he wouldn't have overheard something that impacted so many choices he'd made in his life.

"I was supposed to have been asleep hours ago, but when I heard the shouting and the door slam, I thought something was wrong. In bare feet, I ran down the hall toward my parents' room. I didn't have to put my ear against the door because they were talking loud enough to be heard through the closed door."

He paused as he gathered his thoughts. Part of him wanted to stop here—to shove away the memory that had been troubling him most of his life—but the other part of him needed to say this—to put it out into the universe.

He drew in a deep breath, trying to calm his insides. And then, ever so slowly, he blew out the breath. "I heard my mother say she needed to tell us that my father wasn't the biological father of us all. Some of the words were muffled with her sobs. But then my mother said she'd messed up by having that affair and how guilty she felt." Enzo paused, struggling to keep his emotions in check. "My father told her she couldn't tell us—that we were too young to understand. And then she mentioned me and how I wasn't a little boy any longer. But my father said it wasn't fair to tell me a secret that I couldn't tell my sisters."

Sylvie reached out, placing her hand on his arm. It was a quiet gesture—a caring touch. And it gave him the strength to finish.

"I'm not sure how long I stood there, trying to make sense of what I'd just heard. My mother had an affair. And at the time, I was certain I was the illegitimate child. Why else would she have mentioned my name?"

"It must have been such a shock."

He nodded. "My mind was reeling. I wasn't a Bartolini. I didn't belong."

"Did you approach your parents?"

He shook his head. "I went to bed that night and eventually I fell asleep. In the morning my parents acted totally normal. And being a kid,

I was able to convince myself that it was just a dream. But deep inside I knew it was so much more than a dream."

"And so all of these years you've been dealing with that on your own? Without being able to talk to anyone?"

"But it isn't about me. It's about my sisters. I was too ashamed—too worried about my own feelings—to speak up. But I should have said something. I should have done something."

"You were just a kid. That's a lot to handle."

He raked his fingers through his hair once more. Frustration over his inaction and anger at his lack of courage twisted his gut up in a knot. "I can't hide behind that excuse. I had a chance to speak up when my sisters found that journal. And yet, I kept the awful secret to myself. I didn't think of how it would eat at them—the not knowing."

Sylvie's hand slid down his arm until her fingers brushed over his palm. The sensation sent a sizzling sense of awareness zinging up his arm. Her fingers slipped between his as she squeezed his hand.

"I know your sisters wouldn't blame you for being shocked when the secret came out. It had been years and you'd convinced yourself that it was a dream."

"But I should have said something. I was ashamed that I wasn't a Bartolini. I was scared they wouldn't look at me as their big brother. I didn't want our relationship to change. I thought if I sat on the information that I'd have a little longer until the DNA results revealed the inevitable—I wasn't a biological Bartolini."

"You'd just lost your parents—you were afraid of losing your sisters."

"That's not good enough." He pulled away from her and stood. His gaze drifted to the floor. "If I was a good brother—if I'd have protected my sisters the way my father had always told me to do—I would have spoken up."

Sylvie placed her fingers beneath his chin and lifted until their gazes met. "Maybe you should have spoken up sooner, but what you would have told them would have been misinformation. You are a Bartolini by blood. Perhaps it would have been worse for your sisters believing one thing, only to find out it wasn't the truth."

"But if I'd have had the courage to speak up all those years ago, my parents could have talked to us. They could have explained their actions. Now we're left with guessing at their motives."

"And this is why you're selling the estate? You don't feel that you deserve it?"

He shrugged. "My sisters both moved away and started over. It's time I do the same thing."

"Have you told your sisters all of this?"

He shook his head. "I can't." His sisters were all the family he had in this world. "I can't risk losing them."

"Do you really think that will happen? Because I don't. I know your sisters love you as much as you love them. And nothing will break you apart."

In her gaze he saw truth and compassion, but it wasn't enough to change his mind. "I… I can't do it."

"If you don't, I don't think you'll ever find that fresh start you're seeking, no matter how far you move from here."

He wanted to argue with her. He wanted to tell her that she was wrong. But he didn't. Sylvie was a smart woman, but the risk of revealing his secret to his sisters was too great. They'd already lost so much—been through so much. And he didn't want them to look at him like—like he'd let them down.

"You won't say anything, right?" he asked.

"You know you can trust me. It's not my secret to tell. But for your own sake, you need to tell them."

"I… I have to go."

"Stay." She approached him. "We don't have to talk."

The thought of spending the night getting lost in her sweet, addictive kisses was so very tempting. Every fiber of his body longed to reach out to her and draw her close. But he knew if he did that, he'd never let her go.

And that wouldn't be fair to Sylvie—sweet Sylvie, who believed in true love, happily-ever-afters and the goodness in people. But he could be none of those things to her.

His gaze automatically moved to her lips. Why did it seem like such a natural thing to kiss her good-night? Perhaps it was the same reason he'd entrusted her with his most deeply held secret.

But he just couldn't complicate matters even further. Not after he'd just told her the reason they shouldn't be together. He wasn't a person she could count on because he let down the people he loved.

He raised his gaze to meet hers. "I'll see you in the morning."

Disappointment—or was that pain?—showed in her eyes. In a blink it was hidden behind a blank stare. She didn't say anything as he turned and walked away.

With each step he felt as though he was doing the wrong thing. Sylvie might be the best thing that ever happened to him, but he wasn't the best for her.

CHAPTER NINE

THE DAY COULDN'T have been more beautiful.

The sun was bright. The blue skies were clear. And the air was warm.

But the mood in the car was anything but bright and cheery. The shadows under Enzo's eyes said that he hadn't gotten much sleep, if any. She'd at least drifted off for a few hours but her stomach wasn't feeling the best. She wrote it off as motion sickness. It would soon pass.

After a quiet car ride, they arrived in Florence. Without much sleep, espresso was very tempting. When Enzo repeatedly offered to get her some, her stomach still wasn't up for it.

On her phone, Sylvie did a search of stores in Florence. "There are a lot of shops we can check for decorations."

"Sounds like a plan."

She started reading off the directions. When she looked up, she noticed he'd turned in the opposite direction. "The shops are the other way."

"This is just a little detour."

"But we have to get back to the vineyard and finish setting up."

"Relax. We have time. And you did say you've never taken time to look around the city."

It was true. Since she'd moved from Patazonia, she hadn't spent much time in Florence. Sadly, the few times she'd visited this beautiful and historically rich city, she'd been here to do wedding business and so still hadn't seen much. She'd dreamed of one day taking the time to visit some of the city's sights, but there was always a meeting to attend, a need to rush back to the estate and never enough time to just relax and be a tourist.

The fact he was taking a detour this morning was something she'd wanted for a long time. So why was she fighting it? Why didn't she just let go of her worries and enjoy the day—wherever it led them?

Enzo parked the car. Sylvie stepped out and lifted her face to the morning sun. It warmed her skin and energized her. This was going to be a good day after all. This tour of Florence with Enzo as her guide would be priceless.

"Where are we going to start?" Excitement pumped through her veins.

"This way." He gestured over his shoulder. "I hope you wore your walking shoes."

"I did." She never imagined she would be touring Florence, but she'd dressed to do some serious shopping and that involved a lot of walking.

The people of Florence shared friendly smiles and greetings. They made Sylvie feel as though she fit right in. Enzo started off by telling her that he wasn't a professional tour guide so he wouldn't be able to answer all her questions about the city, but he would do his best. She had no doubt that he was the perfect person to show her the sights.

"Unless you want to take a professionally guided tour," he said. "I'm not sure what time slots are available. Whatever it is, we can make it work. I don't want you to miss out on anything."

Sylvie placed a hand on his forearm. "Stop. I would like you to do the tour, if you're still willing."

He nodded.

They set off, side by side. There was just something about seeing the city through his eyes that appealed to her. And with Enzo's mood improving, the company was the best part of all.

"Our first stop is the Ponte Vecchio Bridge or Old Bridge," Enzo said. "It's one of the oldest bridges in Europe. And it still has houses built on it, though most of them are now shops."

"I can't even imagine living on a bridge." She marveled at the idea.

"There are some great views from there."

They started across the crowded bridge. There was an energy flowing through the crowd as they laughed and talked amongst themselves as well as conversed with the vendors, most of whom were jewelers. She was immediately drawn in by the showcases. She told herself that she was only going to browse. She didn't have any extra money to splurge on any of the dazzling baubles for sale—not when she was about to lose her home and job. But looking didn't cost anything.

She was in awe at some of the remarkable pieces. But there was a necklace of silver and gemstones designed to look like a cluster of purple grapes with green leaves all wired together. It was remarkable. And she loved it. Then she looked at the price. It was too much for her budget. She gave it a lingering glance then, with a resigned sigh, she moved on.

She didn't say anything to Enzo about the necklace, but when he was drawn in by a wristwatch, she backtracked to take a second look at the necklace. She didn't want to explain to Enzo why she couldn't buy it. She didn't want to make him feel guilty over the events at the estate. After all, it was just a necklace—a stunning, handcrafted necklace—but a necklace all the same.

As they continued across the bridge, Sylvie pushed thoughts of the necklace to the back of her mind. It wouldn't change things to dwell on something she couldn't have. However, the memories made today were priceless. She loved everything about her time in Florence—including her tour guide. As soon as the thought came to her, she dismissed it. Where had it come from? She was just letting the excitement of the day and their newfound easiness with each other get to her.

She paused by the bridge's outlook to take in the beautiful view of the river and the surrounding city.

"Wait here," Enzo said. "I'll be right back."

He disappeared into the crowd. She wasn't sure where he was going, most likely tracking down some espresso. A yawn tugged open her mouth. She refused to give in to her tiredness. Today she would take in all the sights. Tonight she could sleep. But right now she didn't intend to miss a thing. Or at least whatever they had time to see.

Enzo returned. "Turn around."

"What?"

"Turn around." When she frowned at him, trying to figure out what he was holding behind his back, he said, "Trust me."

With a bit of trepidation, she did as he asked. He reached around her, placing something on her neck, but he moved so fast that she couldn't get a good look at what was in his hand. For a moment she thought it was the necklace she'd liked so much, but she dismissed the notion. He wouldn't know about it, as she hadn't mentioned it.

But as she reached for the pendant, Enzo

said, "Hold still. I'm having a hard time with this catch." When she stopped moving, he said, "I've almost got it… There we go."

Sylvie moved her long hair, letting the chain rest against her neck. And then she lifted the pendant, finding the stunning mixture of gemstones and wire art. "How did you know?"

When she turned a smile to him, he returned the gesture. "I was hoping for that reaction."

"What reaction?"

"Your smile. It brightens the whole world—at least my entire world."

His words caused her heart to pitter-patter faster. "Thank you so much." She fingered the pendant. "I love it. But you shouldn't have done it. I'll pay you back—"

"No, you won't. That was a gift from me to you."

"But—"

"No buts, just enjoy it. It looks good on you."

They moved on, stopping to visit the bust of goldsmith/sculptor Benvenuto Cellini, where lovers from near and far had visited and affixed hundreds of locks to the fence surrounding the statue. Legend had it if they threw the key in the Arno River, their love would be eternal.

Sylvie wondered about having a love like that—a love like her parents'. She didn't believe it happened for everyone. It wouldn't happen to her, but the thought of having a love that endured time, trials and tribulations was very tempting indeed.

From the bridge, they visited Piazza della Signoria, Florence's town center with its remarkable open-air sculpture gallery with its stunning works of art. There was so much to take in that it couldn't all be done in a day, but they kept moving.

Sylvie snapped photo after photo on her phone. She didn't want to forget a single moment. At the Galleria dell'Accademia, she marveled at all the statues and paintings. However, the sculpture of David by Michelangelo made her pause and admire the level of skill involved. Sylvie never considered herself a fan of Renaissance, but she was starting to change her mind.

With a lull in the crowd, she paused to consider how someone could carve stone with such detail. It was truly amazing. It would definitely take a lot of talent and strength as well as imagination. She wondered if people doubted

Michelangelo's talents in the beginning. Did his parents encourage him to do something more traditional with his life—like blacksmithing? Or did they encourage him to follow his dreams?

She thought of her loving mother, who'd always wanted the best for Sylvie. She'd thought Sylvie had talent designing wedding dresses but believed it took more than talent to make it in this sometimes challenging world they lived in. And so her mother had encouraged her to find a more traditional career. Sylvie had heeded her mother's cautious words, but she couldn't help but wonder what would have happened if she'd been brave and followed her dreams.

Sylvie turned to Enzo. "Thank you for bringing me here. I will never forget this day."

"There's something I've been meaning to say to you and for one reason or another, I've kept putting it off." His sincere gaze met hers. He drew in a visible breath. "I'm sorry for how I acted after Paris. It wasn't right. I tried to blame you and it was so wrong. The truth is the night meant more to me than I was willing to admit. I made every excuse possible to avoid dealing with those feelings. Thank you for not giving up on me and giving me time to get my head screwed on straight."

His words touched her heart, making it flutter in her chest. She wasn't quite sure what he was trying to tell her. A part of her wanted to delve deeper into this subject, but the other part of her didn't want to ruin this moment. As hard as it was for her, she believed it was best for both of them to accept what he was willing to give and not push for more. But that didn't mean she didn't owe him an apology, as well.

"I'm sorry, too." She glanced back at the famous statue as emotions churned within her. "I was freaked out, too, after Paris. I never expected things to go in that direction. And then I thought you were mad at me, which made everything worse." She chanced a glance in his direction. "I don't normally act so bold."

A smile played at the corner of his lips. "I like that bold side of you."

"You do?"

He nodded. "Bold looks good on you."

She smiled, too. His gaze caught and held hers. Her heart pounded in her chest. It was so loud it echoed in her ears. How was it possible this man could have such a powerful draw over her?

"About last night—"

"We were both exhausted," she said. "There's nothing more that needs said about it."

His gaze searched hers. "You don't think less of me?"

"No. I think you're a very caring brother and friend."

And then his gaze noticeably lowered to her lips. Was he going to kiss her right here in front of all these people? She didn't care who watched. All she cared about was being in his arms once more.

Her heart thumped harder and faster with each passing moment. The background faded away. In that moment it was just the two of them—

Someone bumped into Sylvie. She landed against Enzo's muscular chest. Jarred from the magical spell that had been spun over them, Sylvie jumped back. They both turned to find a teenage boy.

"Sorry." The boy's face was flushed.

"Be careful," Enzo warned. "You could have hurt someone."

The boy nodded and moved on, submerged into the crowd.

Enzo turned to her. “Are you all right?”

She nodded as her heart slowed. The stolen moment was over before it’d even begun.

“Come on,” Enzo said, “we need to keep moving. I don’t want you to miss visiting the shops before they close.”

He took her hand in his and moved onward, working their way to the exit. Her hand felt good within his grasp. She refused to define what it meant. A label on this thing happening between them would ruin the moment. It was best just to live in the moment and not analyze it.

CHAPTER TEN

HER FINGERS BRUSHED over the pendant.

A warmth swirled in her chest.

She told herself not to read too much into the friendly gesture. Enzo didn't want attachments—in fact, he was doing his best to minimize his commitments in life with the sale of the estate. She'd do well to remember that. Her hand lowered to her side.

They'd made their way through a number of stores. In a secondhand shop, she found some crystal vases. And then in a florist shop, she found some dried flowers that were stunning. There were vivid reds and deep purples as well as ivory flowers. In addition, she picked out some fresh arrangements. Considering the magazine people would be there the following day, the flowers would just be blooming when she got them home.

She turned to Enzo, who was standing by the door as though anxious to move on. While the sales clerk packed her purchases, Sylvie approached Enzo. He looked totally bored out of his mind.

She held out a fresh bouquet of deep purple and white blooms. “What do you think?”

He shrugged. “They’re fine.”

Not the ringing endorsement she’d been hoping for, but she supposed it’d have to do. “Do you like the other things I picked out?” When he nodded, she asked, “Do you even know what colors I picked?”

“Pink?”

She sighed. For a man who spent most of his time dealing with grapes and vines, his interest certainly didn’t extend to flora and fauna. “No. Reds and purples.”

“Oh. Yeah.”

“Don’t worry, we’re almost done.” And that was when her gaze skimmed past him to the notice just over his shoulder. It was an ad for an apartment.

She initially dismissed it. But as she turned to walk away, she realized Enzo hadn’t given her any real reason to believe he was going to change his mind about keeping the estate. If she didn’t take this situation seriously, she’d end up homeless again. Having gone through that situation once, she wasn't about to let it happen again—especially when she was in a position to prevent it.

She turned back and read the write-up again, paying attention to the details. One bedroom. Pets allowed. The thought of coming home to a dog or cat appealed to her. Her gaze latched on to the rent. It was affordable. Very affordable.

When she realized the apartment was right above the florist, she knew she couldn't leave here until she saw it. The posting said to inquire at the desk and that was exactly what she intended to do.

"I'll be back," she said to Enzo.

"Where are you going?"

"To see an apartment." That was unless it was already taken. She hoped not because it fit in her tight budget. She had a decent amount in savings, but she really hated to rely on it to live. So modesty was the course of action until she secured a job. The next item on her to-do list.

"An apartment? What apartment?"

She didn't stop to answer him. She was a lady on a mission. But she could hear his footsteps behind her. She came to a stop at the checkout counter. The young man who'd been waiting on her was gone, so he likely had stepped into the back.

Enzo leaned close to her. "Why are you interested in an apartment?"

"Why do you think?"

"Well, I know what you do with an apartment, but what I don't understand is why you would want one here. I thought you'd return to Patazonia."

She shook her head. "I don't have any reason to return. My mother was my only family and now that she's gone, I'm on my own. I like it here and I've made some contacts here in Florence. I'm hoping to be able to find a job here."

Enzo grew noticeably quiet. Did he feel bad that she had to search for a new home? It didn't stop her from talking to the young man, who said the apartment was vacant. The sales clerk handed over the key and told them to head upstairs to have a look.

And that was exactly what they did. The apartment wasn't anything fancy, not at all. It was older and could use a fresh coat of paint, but it was clean and with a little work it could be cozy enough.

"You know the kitchen faucet is going to need replaced," Enzo pointed out.

"I'll mention it to the landlord."

"And the bedroom door sticks."

She didn't say anything as Enzo continued to point out the apartment's faults, but all she could see was its possibilities. She needed this to work out. She needed a plan—a way to move forward.

There was a ledge above the kitchen sink where the morning sun would come in. There were small shelves on the walls of the living room where she could place the framed photo of her mother and a picture of her favorite spot by the stream on the Bartolini estate. Little by little she could put her personal stamp on the place, making it feel homey like...like the home she already had in Enzo's guesthouse.

Thoughts of leaving the estate made her sad. She couldn't believe how quickly she'd felt so comfortable there. Maybe it was the country setting or maybe it was her handsome host. Her gaze moved to Enzo as he examined the closet. She was going to miss him—sharing meals with him, morning coffee out on the veranda and their talks.

Tears rushed to her eyes. She blinked them away. She was not a crier, but ever since she'd learned she was losing her home and business, her emotions had been harder to conceal.

"Are you ready to go?" Enzo asked.

She gave the tiny apartment one more look, still not ready to commit to this new future. She nodded her head. "Let's go home."

With the flowers collected and stowed in the car, Enzo drove them back to the vineyard while Sylvie stared out the window at the beautiful scenery. But it wasn't the tall Cypress trees lining the road or the rolling hills that captured her attention; it was the war raging within her between sticking out her plan to convince Enzo to change his mind about the estate or cutting her losses and moving to Florence now. The sooner she got there, the sooner she'd accept the reality of her situation—she had no future with Enzo.

She focused her thoughts on what was awaiting her in Florence. The location of the apartment was superb as it was in the heart of the city. And best of all, it was furnished. Old furniture, but it appeared to be well taken care of. All the money she'd save with the low rent and not having to buy furniture would help stretch her savings until she landed a job.

But she also realized she'd been the one responsible for inviting the magazine to the estate. She had to stay and see this through until the end. And then she would move on—no matter how hard it would be for her.

CHAPTER ELEVEN

THE BIG DAY had arrived.

Praises and compliments were bandied about.

But all Enzo could think about was the small apartment in Florence—where Sylvie was considering living. It was so much smaller than the house on this estate. And it needed a lot of work.

He knew those were all excuses. The truth of the matter was he didn't want her moving there. He didn't want her to be so far away.

And yet, he couldn't ask her to stay here. Because soon, he would no longer own the estate. So what did that leave him? To ask her to move to France with him? Impossible. That would mean strings and commitments, things he was just now untangling himself from with the sale of the estate.

"This is great." The reporter, Jameson Asaro, seemed more interested in smiling at Sylvie than exploring the estate. "I think we have all we need of the villa and vineyard."

"Are you sure?" Sylvie asked.

"You've been an excellent guide." Jameson smiled once more at Sylvie. "I've really enjoyed your company."

Color rose in Sylvie's cheeks. "Thank you."

Unhappy with this conversation, Enzo cleared his throat as he made a point of checking the time on his wristwatch. It was definitely time to move this interview along.

"You know, Enzo's father built all of this," Sylvie said. "Isn't that right, Enzo?"

He knew she was trying to get him to talk. He didn't like this guy or the way he flirted with Sylvie. Still, Sylvie was looking at him expectantly. "Um, yes. That's right. He inherited the land from my grandfather, but until that point, it was just wide-open space." He pressed his hands to his trim waist. "This was all my father's hard work."

The reporter made a note on his digital tablet. "But you have worked on the grapes, right?"

"Yes. I've been instrumental in blending the grapes."

"How did you do that if you were living and working in France?"

"I started the work before I moved to France. And though my father and his crew did the day-to-day maintenance, I came home periodically to oversee things."

"So you and your father must have worked closely together."

Enzo paused, recalling his time with his father. In the beginning his father wouldn't listen to Enzo's ideas. But as the years went by and Enzo gained more experience, his father would actually seek out his advice. It had been the greatest feeling in the world. "We did."

The reporter made a notation in his notes. "Then why move to France? Why not work here with your father?"

"My father believed in everyone learning to be independent."

"So you were planning to return?"

He didn't like the direction of these questions. He never should have agreed to the interview. He didn't want to dissect his life with his father. He didn't want to acknowledge that he'd headed off on his own to learn as much as he could in order to return to the Barto Vineyard and make it bigger and better. And to one day have his father hand over the reins—trusting Enzo with what his father had created and worked his whole life to make thrive.

"Yes." Enzo's voice rumbled with emotion. He slammed the door on those memories. He swallowed hard. "We should get going." He turned for the door. "I've arranged to give you a horseback tour of the estate. It's the only true way to see the place." He paused and turned back to them. "Do you ride?"

The reporter's questions were opening doors to Enzo's past.

But would they be enough to change the course of the future?

Sylvie's breath caught as she waited to see how this would play out. Luckily, both men were agreeable to a horseback ride. She let out the pent-up breath.

In the next breath it struck her that Enzo had planned the horseback tour on his own, without even consulting her. If he didn't care about the estate and was so anxious to get rid of it, would he have gone to the bother? Would he have gone along with any of this?

She didn't think so. As they all got saddled up, she was smiling broadly. Enzo might not be willing to admit it, but he was attached to the estate. Talking about selling it and doing it were two totally different things. When it finally came down to putting pen to paper, she didn't think he could do it.

Once the reporter and photographer were seated on two of the most mellow horses in the stable, Sylvie mounted Duchess at the same time Enzo climbed on Emperor. Off they went. Enzo took the lead and she was curious where he would lead them. It didn't take her long to figure out he was leading them to her favorite spot, next to the stream.

"You own all of this land?" the reporter asked.

"Yes." Enzo didn't expound upon the answer.

Sylvie had taken up the rear, sandwiching their two visitors in between so no one got lost, because there was a lot of land out here in which to wander off in the wrong direction.

"It's very picturesque." Sylvie admired the passing scenery. "I love to come out here when I have time just to take in the quiet beauty and unwind."

"How long have you worked here?" Jameson asked.

"I just started working here this year." And yet, it seemed so much longer. "I immediately fell in love with the estate." And she was pretty crazy about its owner, but she kept that part to herself.

It seemed like she'd been keeping more and more to herself these days. In the beginning of all this, she and Enzo could talk about most anything. It was like they had an immediate rapport—

Whinny!

The next thing she knew Duchess came to an abrupt stop. Before she could think to react, the horse reared up. Sylvie clung tight to the reins and tightened her legs. But gravity was too much for her. She thought she heard Enzo call out her name.

She went airborne.

A scream tore from her lungs.

And then she landed on the hard ground with a thud. The air whooshed from her lungs. And as her head hit the ground, blackness engulfed her, swallowing her whole.

* * *

She just had to be all right.

That was all Enzo could think when he saw Sylvie motionless on the ground. And that was what he thought when she came to and insisted that she was all right. She was more worried about the horse, who'd been spooked, than herself. Against his wishes, she'd gotten to her feet.

It was all he could do to convince her that they were going to the A&E. When he'd pointed out that she'd blacked out momentarily, she'd grudgingly conceded but insisted that no ambulance was necessary. And so he drove her. She was so stubborn.

And now, as they waited in a hospital cubicle, Sylvie grew restless. He couldn't blame her. This place was boring but necessary.

"This is silly to wait around here," Sylvie said. "There's nothing wrong with me."

"That bump on your head would indicate otherwise."

She sighed as though giving up the fight. Because there was no way she was getting out of the hospital until the doctor cleared her.

A few minutes of silence passed between

them. In that time Enzo's mind went to a dark place as he thought about how close he'd come to losing her. The thought of his world without Sylvie in it—well, he couldn't imagine it. Never seeing her bright, sunny smile again or being able to pick up his phone and hear her soft voice and infectious giggle. He halted his troubling thoughts. Thankfully, none of that had happened.

"I'm sorry."

The words were so soft—so faint—that he wasn't sure he heard her correctly. "Sorry?" When she nodded, he asked, "For what?"

"For ruining your interview with the magazine. I can't even imagine what they must think."

He wanted to tell her that he didn't care what they thought. The only important thing was her well-being. But he stopped himself. He told himself that he didn't want to hurt her feelings since she'd arranged for the magazine coverage and worked so hard to make the estate look picture-perfect. He ignored the part about how his admission might convey how much she'd come to mean to him—as a friend, that is.

"Everything is going to work out fine," he

said with a conviction he was lacking because he knew they'd soon be parting ways and—and he'd miss their conversations.

"Ms. DeLuca?" A doctor they hadn't seen before stepped into the cubicle.

"Yes." There was a slight tremor in her voice.

Enzo couldn't help but wonder if she was worried about having to spend the night in the hospital. Before he could reassure her that everything would be all right, the doctor turned to Enzo. The words froze in Enzo's throat.

"I'm Dr. Costa." The older man wearing a white coat held out his hand. "And you would be?"

"Enzo." Suddenly, he felt nervous. What was the doctor going to say? Was there something wrong with Sylvie and that was why a new doctor was here? As the doctor's eyes prompted Enzo for more information, Enzo found his voice once more. "I'm, uh, Sylvie's friend."

The doctor nodded in understanding. "If you could go to the waiting area, I'd like to speak to Ms. DeLuca."

"I'd like him to stay," Sylvie said. "He's never going to believe I'm okay until he hears it from you."

The doctor's bushy white brows drew together behind his silver-framed glasses. "Okay, then."

Would the doctor have asked him to leave the room if nothing was wrong? Enzo didn't think so. And he wanted to be there for Sylvie to lean on if the news wasn't good.

The doctor focused on Sylvie. "You've had quite a fall and you have a slight concussion. Your other tests came out fine. Are you having any cramping?"

Sylvie's eyes showed her confusion. "No."

"Any spotting?"

"Spotting?" Her voice wavered. When the doctor nodded, she said, "No."

"That's good." The doctor smiled at her. "Now, if your friend will step outside, I'll just check and make sure everything is all right with the baby."

The breath hitched in Enzo's throat.

Baby? What baby?

Surely, the doctor was confused. Enzo turned his attention to Sylvie. All the color had leached from her face. Judging by her wide-eyed gaze and her slack jaw, she was as surprised by this diagnosis as he was.

"Just move to the waiting area," the doctor prompted as a nurse rushed in. "We won't be long."

Enzo turned his stunned gaze to Sylvie. He didn't want to walk away. He had questions. Lots of qucstions.

He opened his mouth to say something but his voice failed him.

How had this happened?

That was a foolish question. He recalled very vividly how this had happened. Every last sizzling detail.

The doctor cleared his throat, startling Enzo into action. On wooden legs, he walked away. But not far. Not far at all.

She was pregnant.

It wasn't as big of a shock as Sylvie had expected.

Maybe because way down deep in her subconscious, she'd suspected it. She just hadn't allowed herself to admit it. After all, what were the chances that the first time you make love that you would turn up pregnant?

She didn't think the odds were very high. Leave it to her to be the one in a million. But it explained her symptoms, from her tender breasts, to her upset stomach, to her heightened emotions. And if she were to finally slow down enough to consult her day planner, she'd likely notice that her cycle was late. Inwardly, she groaned. This was the worst timing—the absolute worst.

When the doctor finished his thorough exam, he said, "Everything appears good. But considering the severity of your fall, I'd like to do a transvaginal ultrasound." He went on to explain the procedure to her.

"I'll be able to see the baby?" she asked. Hope and excitement swelled within her chest.

The doctor nodded. "And we should be able to hear its heartbeat." The doctor typed some notes into the computer that was mounted on a cart. "Was that the father who was just in here?"

"Yes." There was no hesitation in her answer because Enzo was the only man in her life, if you could stretch the meaning of being in someone's life.

"Would you like to have him in here for the ultrasound?" When she nodded, the doctor said, "As soon as you're all set up, someone will go get him. The technician should be in shortly."

And then the doctor left her alone. It was quite loud in her head as one thought preceded another. Quite often they were in contradiction of each other. But in the end, they all boiled down to: What was she going to do now?

CHAPTER TWELVE

IT WAS A black screen.

And then some gray lines washed over the monitor.

Enzo squinted, trying to make out the image of a baby—of his son or daughter. That thought momentarily caused the breath to become trapped in his lungs. How was it that he was going to become a father when he hadn't even gotten his own life straightened out?

The technician wearing pink scrubs, with her dark hair pulled up in a messy bun, made some adjustments, clearing up the picture. She pointed to the screen. "There's your baby."

Sylvie gasped. And then she sniffled and swiped at her cheeks. "Can you tell if it's a boy or girl?"

"It's too early. That will happen in your second trimester."

Sylvie turned to Enzo with a teary smile.

"It's so small. I… I hope I didn't hurt him or her in the fall."

Enzo wanted to reassure her that everything would be all right, but he couldn't make her that promise. Instead, he reached out and took her cold hand in his. He rubbed his thumb over the back of her hand.

"Would you like to hear the heartbeat?" the technician asked.

"Oh, yes. Please." The excitement rang out in Sylvie's voice.

A new sense of guilt settled over Enzo. After the way his own family had crashed and burned, he was scared to be responsible for a baby. What if he messed up?

Sylvie squeezed his hand, drawing him back to the present. A rapid *swoosh-swoosh* filled the air.

"That's your baby's heartbeat," the technician said. "A baby's heart beats more rapidly than an adult's."

For the moment Enzo halted his rambling thoughts and focused on his son or daughter's heartbeat. The *swoosh-swoosh* drove home the reality of this situation.

He and Sylvie were having a baby.

This shouldn't be happening. The timing was all wrong. The situation was wrong. And his being a father was all sorts of wrong.

Pregnant. Baby.

The words echoed in Enzo's mind during the ride home. It had been a particularly quiet ride as he tried to come to terms with the events of the day. He wasn't the only quiet one. Sylvie had barely said a word since they got in the car. Was she as stunned as he was? Or had she known all along? Was that why she'd been so excited to hear the baby's heartbeat?

He hadn't needed to ask Sylvie if the baby was his. The fact she'd been a virgin until their night in Paris was enough to answer his question. Things had gotten out of control that night. Obviously, mistakes had been made. Big mistakes.

And now he had no idea what to do.

He opened the door of the guesthouse. She walked past him because she refused to let him carry her—even though he'd tried to do just that. She insisted when the doctor said she was to rest for a couple of days that it didn't mean she couldn't walk. She was so stubborn.

Once inside, she refused to go to bed and instead settled on the couch. He sat with her. He rubbed his palms over his jeans. Unable to get comfortable, he jumped to his feet. He started to pace.

He had questions, lots of questions. But he didn't know if now was the right time to ask them. In fact, it probably wasn't the time. He kept his mouth shut and his feet moving over the hardwood floor.

"Ask me," she said.

He stopped and turned to her. "What?"

"You want to ask me about the baby, so go ahead. And yes, the baby is yours."

"How long have you known?" His gaze searched hers as though he could tell if she was lying or not.

"I didn't. I swear. I just found out when you did."

He raked his fingers through his hair. "This… It changes everything."

She glanced down, smoothing out a nonexistent wrinkle in her blouse. "I don't want it to sway your decision."

"What decision?" Was she referring to their relationship? Or had she already skipped ahead to marriage and living happily ever after? Because that had never crossed his mind. Well, not really. Maybe once or twice. But that was it.

Frown lines etched her eyes. "I don't want you to keep the estate out of a sense of obligation."

He didn't say anything. Once more he started to pace. He had a lot to think over before they continued this discussion. There was so much to consider.

"Enzo, I'm sorry."

He stopped. His gaze sought out hers. "Sorry for what?"

"For further complicating your life."

He believed her. He really did. But he didn't blame her. He blamed himself. And right now he couldn't give her the words of reassurance she wanted to hear. He needed time to think.

"We'll talk tomorrow," he said, glancing away. "It's getting late. Do you want anything to eat?"

She shook her head. "I'm fine."

He'd gotten them some takeaway at the hospital while they waited for the test results to come back. It'd taken a while because he insisted the doctors check her thoroughly. He had to be certain she and the baby were all right.

Sylvie stood as though to head for the door. "I'll just let you out."

He shook his head. "I'm not going anywhere."

"What?"

His gaze met hers. "I'm sleeping right here on the couch."

"But…but it's too small for you."

He crossed his arms, refusing to budge. "It'll be just fine. And I want to be close by in case you need anything. After all, you have a concussion."

"A slight one."

"But one all the same."

She opened her mouth as though to argue but then she closed her mouth and walked away. Apparently, she wasn't up for a fight she wasn't going to win.

He resumed pacing and thinking. There wasn't a tired bone in his body. He was totally wound up. He was going to be a father. They were going to be parents. Sylvie was the mother of his baby. The image of her holding a baby filled his chest with a warm, fuzzy sensation.

Sylvie returned, interrupting his daydream. She placed a blanket and pillow on the couch. "You'll need these."

"Thank you. But I'm the one who should be waiting on you."

"I'm fine." Her hand moved to her abdomen. "We're fine. I promise."

She turned and walked away. He wanted to go after her. He wanted to pull her into his arms and hold her close, reassure himself that she was truly fine. But he didn't move. He didn't have the right to touch her—even if she was carrying his baby.

His feet resumed their motion. His gaze moved about the room, coming to rest on a mannequin in the corner of the room. The light from the lamp caught the beads and sequins, making them glitter. It was new to the room. He was drawn to it.

He moved around the armchair that was blocking his full view. And then he realized it was a wedding dress. At first, he assumed it was just part of the wedding business, but a closer inspection revealed that the dress was in the process of being sewn.

What was it doing here? The business bought

dresses, not created them. And if this dress was a part of the business, it would be in the front rooms, in the space dedicated to the business, not back here in Sylvie's private rooms.

What in the world? Was Sylvie making her own wedding dress? But why? To marry whom? Him? The breath hitched in his throat. That couldn't happen.

But there was a baby to consider—their baby. Still, didn't Sylvie understand he wouldn't make a good husband? He'd end up hurting her without meaning to.

CHAPTER THIRTEEN

THE NIGHT HAD been restless.

And the morning wasn't much better as Sylvie hurt everywhere, including a few spots she hadn't known existed. But she refused to let that get her down. The fact the baby was safe was the balm she needed to get up and get moving.

The baby.

Those two life-altering words kept playing over and over in her mind. She knew she should be shocked and scared, and she was, but there was also a sense of awe.

She placed a hand to her still-flat abdomen. It was so hard to believe there was a little baby in there. But it was true. She'd seen it with her own eyes. And Enzo had witnessed it, too.

Enzo.

What was he thinking? Last night he'd looked like the earth had moved out from under his feet. She had no idea what mood he'd be in today.

Knowing there was no point delaying the inevitable, she took a quick shower and dressed. When she stepped out of the bedroom, she was surprised to find Enzo rushing around her small kitchen. He didn't seem to notice her. And so she took in the moment. He looked very busy with whatever he was cooking. From the mess of dirty dishes on the table and counter, she'd hazard a guess that cooking wasn't something he'd mastered.

Not wanting to be caught staring, she moved on. In the small living room, she reached for her digital tablet. She wanted to see the teaser the magazine had planned to post online prior to the release of the magazine.

After all, that was the reason she'd been on horseback. She just hoped it was a glowing article. Perhaps it'd help Enzo's mood. Maybe he'd see possibilities for the future that he'd been unwilling to accept before.

But when she pulled up the online magazine, the first thing to come up on the screen was a horrific photo of a fire—a wildfire. Her gaze caught the headlines: "Burning Inferno."

She went on to read that the fire was a ways away from the Bartolini estate. They weren't sure yet how it'd started, but so far there was zero containment. Sylvie's heart ached for all the destruction and the danger to humans and wildlife. It was an utter nightmare. Hopefully, they'd get it under control quickly.

Under the circumstances, she assumed the article about the vineyard would be sidelined for now, but that didn't keep her from scrolling down over the page.

Near the bottom of the webpage, she spotted a photo of herself and Enzo. What in the world was she doing in the photo? It wasn't anything they'd posed for as she'd made sure to stay out of the camera's range. But there they were among the vines, staring into each other's eyes. The picture made it appear as though they were lovers and that just wasn't the case—not since Paris.

She couldn't even recall this moment, and if Enzo was staring lovingly into her eyes, she'd think she would remember it. All she could figure was that it was a fleeting moment made to appear as something more. Beneath the photo was a headline that caught and held her attention: "Italian Billionaire Off the Market?"

She gasped.

"Sylvie, what's the matter?" Enzo's voice came from behind her. "Is it the baby?"

The next thing she knew Enzo was standing next to her. She pressed the tablet to her chest as she shook her head. What was the point of hiding it from him? He was bound to find out soon enough. With great reluctance, she handed him her tablet with the write-up about them as a couple.

Between news of the wildfire and then the sensationalized headline, her stomach churned. She moved to the couch and sat before her legs gave out. Things were spinning out of control faster than she could deal with them.

When Enzo turned to her, she couldn't read the emotions in his tired, bloodshot eyes. She swallowed hard, insisting her stomach calm itself. Not that it would listen to her.

"I'm sorry." Her voice cracked with emotion. "I… I had no idea they were in this to make sensationalized headlines. If I'd known, I never would have agreed to the visit." Her gaze fell to her hands. "I thought I was helping."

Enzo sat beside her. "This isn't your fault. This is totally on that reporter's shoulders."

"You're not mad at me?"

"About the interview and this write-up? No."

She noticed how he singled out the article, but he hadn't said anything about the baby. She couldn't stand the unknown. She needed to know where they stood. "And the baby? Are you mad at me?"

"Did you intentionally get pregnant?" His gaze searched hers, as though seeking out the truth.

"No. I wouldn't do such a thing."

"Then there's no reason to be mad at you. But I am mad at myself for letting things get out of control and putting us both in this difficult position."

She reached out to him, touching his arm. "You can't take on all of the blame. I started everything by kissing you."

Pain and regret were evident in his eyes as he pulled away from her touch. "But I shouldn't have acted on it. This is all my fault—"

"Stop." Her voice was firm. "We aren't going to play the blame game. What's done is done.

We just have to figure out how to move forward."

Enzo sighed as he rubbed the back of his neck. "You're right. Why don't we start with breakfast?"

"Not yet. We haven't finished talking."

"Just tell me what you want me to do."

"I don't expect anything from you."

"Except not to sell the estate." Enzo frowned. "What I don't get is why you care so much if I keep this place or not."

"Because there's something about this estate…an ease…a hominess…that draws me in. It's so easy to imagine all the happy memories within the walls of the main house. It's something a lot of people strive for all of their lives. But you have it all, right here."

"What I have is a house of lies. Looking back, I can't tell what was true and what was just a well-crafted lie by my parents. This house is where I let down my sisters. It is my biggest failure."

She paused, considering her next words. "After my mother died, I lost our house. I was so far behind in the payments that it was only the bank's goodwill that let my mother stay there until the end. But after that I was out the door. I was homeless. I never knew where I was going to sleep. But thanks to some amazing friends, I only spent a night or two without a roof over my head."

"You never told me that before."

She glanced down at her clasped hands. "I've never told anyone. It's not something I'm proud of."

That made him stop short. His gaze met hers. "You have nothing to be ashamed of. In fact, everything you did for your mother took incredible strength and love. It didn't end the way you wanted but you did a remarkable thing."

Heat rushed to her cheeks. He made it sound like she did something other people in her position wouldn't have done. She didn't think that was the case.

"Thank you but I just did what I had to do."

The wedding was over.

The guests were gone.

And the villa had been put back to rights.

Late Saturday afternoon, Sylvie was exhausted. Even though it had been an intimate morning wedding with just family and close friends, there had still been an abundance of details to see to. It was a bittersweet moment for her as the wedding had been a smashing success, but it was also the last wedding she'd ever hold on the Bartolini estate.

With this mix of emotions churning within her, she felt restless. She needed some fresh air. A stroll would give her a chance to sort out all she needed to do once she moved to Florence. Because come the morning, whether she wanted to or not, it was time to move on—without Enzo.

He'd be there for the baby, of that she didn't doubt, but he wouldn't be there for her, not like the close friend he'd come to be over this past year. And maybe that was for the best. Because if she truly let a man into her life, she needed him to be there out of love, not obligation.

With her trusty bag slung over her shoulder, Sylvie made her way to the stable. The earthy scents of the hay and horses, which may be a turnoff to some, grounded her. She craved that sense of peace today.

One of her passions she'd gained since moving to the estate was horseback riding. As a child she'd always dreamed of having her own horse, but living in the city made owning a horse an expensive challenge—money her mother didn't have.

She moved to Duchess's stall. Immediately, the horse moved to greet her. If a horse could smile, Duchess would be doing so now as she nuzzled Sylvie's hand, urging her to fuss over the horse.

Whenever Sylvie went riding, it was always Duchess she selected. The mare was gentle and patient. In fact, this was the horse Sylvie had learned to ride on when she'd first arrived in Tuscany. But sadly, they wouldn't be able to take one last ride together.

"I'm sorry, girl." Sylvie ran her hand down over the mare's neck. "We can't go riding because I'm having a baby."

Duchess was the second to hear her news. The words felt so strange as they crossed her lips. She was still getting used to this new reality.

The horse studied her with those big golden-brown eyes. And then Duchess whinnied as though to say she understood.

"I'm going to miss you."

With a heavy heart, Sylvie walked away.

Duchess put up a fuss, banging on her stall. She didn't want to be left behind. The horse's displeasure tugged on Sylvie's heart.

Today the stables didn't give her the comfort she'd been craving. Still feeling restless, Sylvie continued walking. With no particular destination in mind, she kept putting one foot in front of the other.

The sun was sinking toward the horizon when Sylvie came to a stop at her favorite spot on the estate. The small stream snaked its way along the edge of the estate. And in the background was a beautiful view of the rolling hills.

With autumn not far off, evenings arrived earlier and earlier. Sylvie wasn't ready to let go of this summer—this magical and amazing season. Who'd have thought she'd have an opportunity to visit Paris? The City of Love had been on her bucket list as well as visiting the Eiffel Tower and now she'd done both—and not alone.

She'd swear that city cast a spell over its visitors—she was convinced of it. Otherwise, how else could she explain her being so bold with Enzo—starting something that spun totally and deliciously out of control?

Now that they were back in Tuscany, she could see things clearer. It was abundantly obvious to her that they didn't belong together. Where he wanted to wipe away the past—pretend it didn't exist, she wanted to cling to it so as not to make the same mistakes. Where he acted hastily, such as deciding to sell the estate, she liked to mull things over and make a plan. Whereas he was stubborn and refused to admit when he'd made a mistake, she accepted her mistakes while trying to do better.

She grabbed the blanket from her bag and smoothed it out in front of a large rock. It was there that she sank down and leaned back. For a moment she took in the beauty of the scenery from the slow-moving stream to the lingering sunshine peeking through the branches of trees on the other side of the stream to the blue sky with the puffy white clouds. She wished she could draw landscapes because this was a sight that should be replicated and shared.

She withdrew her sketch pad from her bag along with her set of drawing pencils. She flipped open her sketch pad and stared down at the wedding dress she was designing. Drawing was something she'd started to do as a child.

She'd loved to draw and color princess dresses, big and puffy. Some had fairy wings. And others were more sci-fi.

But as she grew older, her drawings grew more refined and a lot more realistic. Still favoring a fairy-tale dress over the more everyday dresses, she morphed to wedding dresses. In her mind it seemed to be a natural move for her. At first, her drawings had been of dresses that already existed. The detail work of a wedding dress took a lot of studying and a lot of discarded pages. But eventually she started working on dresses of her own design. At first, they had basic lines and decorative traits. But eventually, she learned to trust her imagination and her skills.

Once she had some original drawings, she used the skills her mother gave to her. Her mother was a seamstress—one of the best in all of Patazonia. Her mother would even give her some helpful hints, but while her mother realized her daughter's real talent, she tried to talk her into more traditional work such as being a seamstress. Her mother didn't believe a nobody like Sylvie would ever make it designing her own fashions, no matter how pretty they were.

She knew her mother had the best of intentions. Sylvie agreed with her. Who would want to buy her fashions? But that didn't keep Sylvie from spending her free time doing the one thing she'd been doing since she was a little girl—back in the days when she thought anything was possible—designing wedding dresses. Though these days it was rare when she had time to devote to her hobby. Today was one of those rare days.

And knowing there wasn't much time before the shadows would grow long and she'd need to head back, she started moving her pencil over the heavy white paper. In no time she was caught up in what she was doing.

A line here. A button there. A plunging neckline. Erase. Erase. A not so plunging neckline. A layer of lace over the bodice. A fitted waistline with a sash of satin. This was definitely one of her favorite dresses by far. And maybe that was why it was taking her the longest to complete. She wanted everything to be perfect—

"Sylvie?"

Her heart lurched straight into her throat. She jumped. Her pencil skidded across the page. As her heart pounded, she turned to find Enzo alighting from his black stallion, Emperor.

"Sylvie, is everything all right?" Enzo approached her. "You look like you just saw a ghost."

It took her a moment to regain the use of her voice. "I'm fine. I was just so caught up in…" She hesitated. She hadn't shared this part of her life with him. "In thought."

"Sorry. I didn't mean to scare you." He sent her a guilty smile.

It was so hard to stay upset with him when he looked at her that way. "It's okay. What did you need?"

"I heard you were at the stables and then you just disappeared. I… I wanted to check on you. And I knew Emperor would enjoy a ride. But I can leave if you want me to."

"No." The word was out of her mouth before she had a chance to decide if their spending alone time was a good idea or not.

After all, there wasn't another soul around. It was once again just the two of them. Why did that conjure up all the wrong thoughts?

CHAPTER FOURTEEN

NOTHING ROMANTIC WAS going to happen.

Enzo already made it quite clear he wasn't interested.

Sylvie moved to the side of the blanket. Enzo joined her. He glanced over at her sketch pad. She'd forgotten all about its still being open. Her initial instinct was to close it, but it would seem rude and she wouldn't do that to Enzo.

As Enzo studied her sketch, she studied him. She wondered if their baby would be a boy or girl. She liked the idea of having a little boy—the spitting image of his father. Her heart filled with love.

And Enzo's dark brown eyes were unforgettable. Would the baby inherit his father's penetrating gaze? Or would they inherit her nothing-special lighter brown eyes? Would their son or daughter be tall like their father? Short like her? Or fall somewhere in between? She had so many questions.

Sylvie wondered if Enzo was curious about their child. They might not have worked as a couple but that didn't mean she didn't want him in their child's life.

In fact, after not knowing her father at all, Sylvic was quitc anxious for Enzo to bc an active part of their child's life, which was another reason she wished he'd change his mind about selling the estate. She'd heard him say in the past that if he didn't live here that he'd probably move back to France. And that was so far away that he'd only see their child once in a while. Not nearly enough for a close relationship.

"Sylvie?" Enzo waved his hand in front of her face. When she blinked and focused on him, he asked, "Did you hear anything I just said?"

"Umm..." Heat rushed to her cheeks. "Sorry. I guess I zoned out. That wedding this morning might have had a small guest list but there were a lot of little details and I'm more tired than I thought."

"Then we should get you back to the house. The doctor said you should take it easy for a few days."

"It has been a few days and I'm fine." When he frowned at her, she said, "Besides, these are the last lingering days of summer and I want to enjoy them before they're gone."

"There's always next year."

"But things will be so different then."

"You mean the baby?"

"Partly." She glanced away. "It's complicated."

He glanced back at her sketch pad. "I didn't know you were artistic."

"I… I'm not. This is just a sketch. It's no big deal."

"It's a huge deal. Call it what you want but that's a definite piece of art. Wow! You're talented."

Heat rushed back to her cheeks. She wasn't used to people complimenting her sketches. "Thank you."

"May I have a closer look?"

She handed over her sketchbook. She wasn't sure why he was making such a big deal of it. She didn't think her sketches were that good and maybe that was why she couldn't finish this dress. In her mind the dress was magnificent, but when she attempted to transfer that image to paper it didn't come out quite the way she imagined.

Enzo held up her sketch and really studied it for a moment. "Do you have more of these?"

She nodded.

"May I look at those, too?"

She nodded once more. She never knew just how exposed she would feel by sharing her sketches with someone. It was like they were looking at a piece of her soul. It was all bare and open for their inspection. And if they didn't like it—if Enzo didn't like what he saw—it would hurt. It would hurt a lot.

He turned page after page. Some were close-ups of the bodice with all the lacework or beading. Others were full dress sketches. She drew what she thought she'd need in order to take the drawing and turn it into a full-fledged dress.

"This is so impressive."

"It's not that good."

His gaze momentarily lifted, meeting hers. "Yes, it is." Then he glanced back at the sketch pad. "Why do you plan weddings instead of designing dresses?"

She shook her head, dismissing such a ridiculous notion. In her mind she heard the echo of her mother's voice: *No matter how good you are, you're still a nobody.*

"It's just a hobby."

He was quiet for a moment as he turned the page. He lifted the sketch pad closer to his face, inspecting each minute line and swirl. "Wait. Is this why you have a wedding dress in your living room?"

"It is. But it's not finished."

"Is it the first one you've sewn?" When she shook her head, he asked, "May I see the other one?"

"I no longer have them."

"Them?" He sounded surprised. "You made more than one?"

"I did."

"What happened to them?"

"I sold them." She lowered her gaze to the striped pattern on the blanket. She could feel him staring at her expectantly.

This part of herself she didn't share with others. Part of the reason she didn't talk about it was the associated pain with that trying time in her life, and the other was the sadness with having to part with her very first wedding dress.

"I get the feeling you didn't do it voluntarily."

She shook her head. What would it hurt to tell him? After all, she'd been privy to much of the drama after his parents' sudden deaths. "I had to sell them in order to pay my mother's medical bills."

"Oh. I'm sorry to push."

"It's okay. I don't talk about it much but it's not a secret." She said this much; she might as well tell him the rest. "When my mother was sick, I worked at a wedding boutique. They sold dresses and accessories as well as planned the weddings." She paused as the painful memories came flooding back.

"And that's how you got the job of working with Bianca?"

"Yes. I worked my way up in the business, but I never learned who recommended me to the royal palace."

"I can see why they did. You're very organized and great with people."

"I try. It's not always easy."

"But your true talent is here." He pointed to her sketch pad. "You put so much of yourself into those dresses. It must have been horrible to part with them."

"It was, but I'd do it again to help someone I love. I can create a new dress, but it's people who are irreplaceable." And if her mother was here right now, she'd be able to show her that you don't have to settle. Sylvie was making a name for herself in the wedding world.

"I'm sorry," he said. "I didn't mean to upset you."

"It's not your fault." She blinked. "I'm fine. I was just thinking about my mother. I feel like I let her down."

"I'm sure you didn't. You have a heart of gold and I'd be willing to bet this entire estate that you did everything you could for her and she knew it, too."

Sylvie glanced down and picked a piece of lint from her jeans. "I just feel bad that when she was so sick, I couldn't be with her all of the time. I had to continue working in order to pay the bills and keep a roof over our heads."

"That couldn't have been easy, feeling like you were being torn in two directions."

"I made sure to have the neighbors stop in and check on her. When the time came, I set up a schedule so there'd always be someone with her."

Enzo reached out and placed his hand over hers. He gave it a squeeze. "You know we have something in common."

She didn't move her hand, taking comfort in the warmth of his touch. She turned her head, finding he was much closer than she'd thought. "What's that?"

"I feel as though I failed my sisters. After our parents died, I was supposed to protect them—make it easier for them. And yet, I did the exact opposite."

"Have you talked to them? Told them your secret?"

He glanced away. "I can't. They'll never understand."

"Give them a chance. They might surprise you."

His gaze met hers. "Why do you care?"

Her heart beat faster. She wondered if he suspected that she had feelings for him. Heat crept up her neck, warming her cheeks. "I don't think you'll ever be able to forgive yourself and make peace with the past without being honest with your sisters."

"Maybe. Maybe not. But telling them is too

big of a gamble. I couldn't take it if they never spoke to me again."

Sylvie reached out and gave his hand a quick squeeze. "They love you. That won't change."

"But I could have done more..."

"You did your best. And that's all anyone can do."

When he gazed at her, his eyes were filled with agony. His pain was so palpable that it sliced into her heart. No wonder he'd decided to sell the estate. He was trying to get away from the pain.

And in that moment all she wanted to do was to comfort him. Without thinking of how her actions could complicate their already messy relationship, she leaned to the side. And there he was. His lips were so close to hers.

He didn't move. She didn't even think he was breathing at this point. The breath hitched in her own throat. She tilted her chin upward and pressed her lips to his.

There was no room in the moment for things to move slowly because the air between them was charged with emotion—deep, raw emotion. And that came through in their kiss. His lips moved over hers with a need she'd never experienced before. And she was there for him, meeting his kiss with a need of her own. She had missed him. Even though they'd coexisted on the same estate, they'd never been farther apart. Until now.

She reached a hand out to him, wrapping her fingers around the back of his neck and then letting her fingers comb up through his thick, dark hair. She shouldn't be doing this. She'd promised herself that whatever they'd shared was over. It was best to keep things simple, but they were not simple right now. Not at all.

In this moment things were hot and getting hotter. And all thoughts of reason had totally escaped her. She was caught up in comforting Enzo and perhaps herself, too. Because as much as she tried to tell herself that she would be all right if the estate was sold, the thought of losing her home again was dredging up excruciating memories of the past when she didn't have a home.

But here in the fading sun with Enzo kissing her, the pain of the past and the worry of the future didn't matter so much. All that mattered in this moment were he and she.

As their kiss intensified, she felt as though

she were floating above the ground. She leaned back against the blanket, drawing him with her. He followed her until her back was pressed upon the blanket. He leaned over her, giving her his full attention—oh, what attention.

A whinny followed by the pounding of hooves caused Enzo to pull away with a frustrated groan. He stared over her shoulder, in the direction of Emperor.

"Is something wrong?" she asked.

"Doesn't appear to be. Emperor must be growing bored." Enzo sat back and held out a hand to help her up. When she was fully upright, he said, "Sylvie, I've decided not to sell the estate. I tried to phone the buyer, but I wasn't able to reach him. I'll tell him when he arrives tomorrow."

Sylvie shook her head. "Don't do it."

"What's that supposed to mean? Aren't you the one who's been waging a campaign to convince me to call off the sale?"

"Would you have changed you mind about selling the estate if there wasn't a baby?"

Enzo averted his gaze and remained silent.

That was all the answer she needed. As hard as she'd tried to remind him what this estate meant to him—to his family—she'd failed. And now there was only one thing for her to do.

"You should sell the estate." Speaking these words was like an out-of-body experience for her. "It's what you intended to do all along. I don't want you to keep it and later blame me or the baby because you feel trapped here."

Enzo was silent for a moment as though absorbing her words. "And if I do sell the place, where will you go?"

"I'm moving to Florence. I'm taking that apartment above the florist."

"But, Sylvie, you can't. This is your home."

She shook her head. "Not any longer. With today being my last wedding and the buyer showing up tomorrow, I don't see a reason for me to put off moving to the city and starting my search for a new job."

Two deep lines formed between Enzo's brows. In his eyes, she could see the wheels of his mind spinning. She didn't know what he was thinking, but whatever it was wouldn't change her mind about leaving.

He visibly swallowed. "Don't go."

"What?" Surely, she hadn't heard him correctly.

"Don't leave. Not yet."

"You want me to stay here and watch you make the biggest mistake of your life?" She shook her head. "I can't do that. My leaving now while things are still amicable between us is what's best for everyone."

His darkened gaze narrowed on her. "I'm glad you've figured out what's best for everyone because I sure haven't." And with that, Enzo stood and, without another word, he strode over to Emperor. With the pounding of hooves, he rode away.

Tears stung her eyes. In truth, she couldn't bear to see the estate sold. For the first time since her mother died, Sylvie truly felt at home. And it was with a very heavy heart that she would leave here.

But she'd reinvented herself after her mother passed on and she would do it again. Her gaze moved to the sketch pad on the blanket. She would find a job as a seamstress. It was steady, reliable work. She definitely preferred a job in the background instead of dealing with nervous brides and anxious mothers.

She sighed. It was for the best. Her baby was counting on her to provide a steady, loving home—not one full of drama. Love was fleeting. Hadn't she been taught that lesson over and over?

Her mother and father had a fleeting love. Her mother used to say that it burned so bright, so hot, that it'd burned itself out. Theirs had been a love-at-first-sight scenario. They were engaged in a month and married within six months of meeting. Her mother had been pregnant with Sylvie a month later. Everything in their relationship was rush-rush. Looking back now, Sylvie supposed that was just her mother's nature, always rushing here and there until cancer struck her down and trapped her in bed. Sylvie shoved aside the painful image.

Her parents' love had been short, but her mother swore that it was one of those loves that was so all-encompassing that she would never love anyone else the way she'd loved Sylvie's father. Sylvie never understood what her mother had meant, but she was starting to get an idea because that night she'd spent with Enzo, from dinner at the awards ceremony, to visiting the Eiffel Tower, to strolling through

Paris, to winding up in his arms that night, had been like a love affair in fast-forward motion. It all went by so fast and now all she had were the memories.

No. That wasn't exactly true. She had their baby.

And unlike her father, who died in a work-related accident just short of her parents' first anniversary—Enzo was healthy and would go on to live a long life. She had to believe it.

She couldn't help but think of how her mother had gotten sick just as Sylvie had finished school—just when she'd made it through her turbulent teen years. She and her mother had just found solid ground when her mother had received her diagnosis.

It was around that time when Sylvie had met a guy, not just any guy, but someone she thought she could get serious with, but as soon as her mother was diagnosed, he was gone. It was then that Sylvie had accepted that she could only count on herself. It was a hard-learned lesson and one she shouldn't forget.

And that was why she needed to end things here with Enzo. No more kisses. No more physical contact of any sort because where they were concerned one thing just naturally led to another and that wasn't helping either of them.

No more excuses. No more delays. It was time she left once and for all.

CHAPTER FIFTEEN

SYLVIE WAS GONE.

It was for the best.

No matter how many times Enzo told himself that it didn't feel like it was for the best. Still, it wasn't like he couldn't drive to visit her whenever he wanted. After all, when the estate was sold, he'd be moving, too. But now with news of the baby, he was rethinking his plans to move to France. That was a lot farther from Sylvie and the baby than he wanted to be.

But the problem was that she'd moved before they'd had time to sort out the future and make arrangements concerning the baby. He'd wanted to stop her from leaving, but what did he have to offer her? His life was in disarray. He didn't even know where he'd be sleeping next month.

After weather delays, the buyer, Mr. Renezo, had arrived a day late and had enjoyed everything about the estate—that was before the winds and wildfire took a distinctive turn. The fire was creeping toward the Bartolini estate—Enzo's home. Firefighting efforts were hampered by wind gusts that jumped fire lines.

In the wine-tasting room, Enzo had just sat down with Mr. Renezo and their attorneys to sign the sale papers. Enzo hadn't eaten that day. His stomach was bothering him. He blamed it on his nagging headache. All of Sylvie's reasons for him not to sell kept nagging at him.

Though the wildfire troubled Mr. Renezo, he was still willing to buy the estate so long as the fire didn't touch the property. That was a big *if* and they both knew it. But since the man had taken time from his busy schedule to fly in, they were ironing out the details.

The problem was that Mr. Renezo didn't want to keep the estate as it was. The man planned to destroy many of the buildings Enzo's father had built, including the little house where Sylvie had stayed. Even the main house wouldn't be recognizable when this man was done. Any memory of Enzo's family would be wiped away.

Part of Enzo realized when the sale was complete that it was Mr. Renezo's property to do with as he pleased, but the other part of him couldn't reconcile himself to the fact that his childhood home would no longer exist as he'd always known. When he'd started down this road, he'd never realized just how difficult it was going to become.

Needing a break from answering Mr. Renezo's questions, Enzo headed outside the winery. A hint of smoke hung in the air. There was no escaping it.

Another of his father's bits of wisdom came to him: *Change doesn't come easily but it's necessary.* Enzo just had to keep moving forward until the deal was complete. Everything would work out then. Wouldn't it?

Vito came rushing up to him. His tanned face was marred with deep worry lines. Enzo's heart sank down to his work boots. Had the fire reached the Bartolini property?

"How bad is it?" Enzo's words were rushed.

"It's bad. Do you have room for another family?" Vito asked. He'd returned early from his holiday when he heard about the fire.

Enzo raked his fingers through his hair. With evacuation orders up in the area, he'd been taking in displaced families. After all, he had an unoccupied hotel. He might as well put it to good use. The only problem was that it had filled up quickly.

"Put them in my room," he said. "I'll grab what I need and bunk down here with the rest of the crew." Vineyard workers who didn't have a family of their own was camping here, ready to do whatever was necessary.

Besides, now that Sylvie was gone, he spent as little time in the main house as possible. The estate was so empty, even with all these people staying here. Nothing was the same without Sylvie's bright smile and bubbly laugh.

With a resigned sigh Enzo turned toward the door. It was time to go back inside and sign the sales agreement—if the wildfire didn't incinerate the estate first.

Mr. Renezo looked up from the papers in front of him when Enzo entered the room. His silver hair was trimmed very short, revealing his lack of hair atop his head. From behind his silver frames his sharp gaze studied Enzo. "Everything all right?"

Enzo nodded. At least for the moment. "We should get the sales agreement signed."

"Just remember I've had my attorney write in

a clause that if the wildfire destroys the property that this agreement is null and void, so if your rushing to sign is some sort of idea that you'll sign it and be off the hook if the worst happens, think again."

"The idea never crossed my mind. Let's do this." Enzo needed to get this over with, the sooner the better. Because the longer they took, the more the doubts about his actions circled overhead, weighing on him.

As he lifted the pen, he saw Sylvie's image in his mind. She was frowning at him and shaking her head in disapproval. But she didn't understand. No one understood that this place represented his failures—the secret his parents kept—the secret he'd hid.

It was best to forget the past and just get on with the future. A fresh start that included a baby. Sylvie and his baby. He would do better by their child. There would be no secrets—secrets that shook the foundation of their family.

As they were about to sign the sales agreement, Vito rushed into the room. He didn't apologize for his presence. And by the distinct paleness of his face, it was clear that things had gotten worse.

He moved to Enzo's side. Vito leaned over and whispered, "We have to go. The fire is headed right for us."

In that moment Enzo wondered if this was his punishment for all the mistakes he'd been making with his sisters, with the estate—with Sylvie. Was the choice to stay or go being taken out of his hands? Was his past about to go up in smoke?

In the next breath he realized he wasn't a quitter. He refused to let the flames of fate take the decision of whether he should stay or go out of his hands.

He would stop the fire—he hoped. He would protect this land that had been left to him—that was so rich in memories. Some good. Some not so good.

And then he thought of Sylvie. She was always lurking at the edge of his thoughts. This estate is where he'd first met her. For whatever reason, she loved this place. And that was all the reason he needed to do whatever needed to be done.

CHAPTER SIXTEEN

THIS COULDN'T BE HAPPENING.

Sylvie glanced out the window of the Bartolini estate. The whole villa had been closed up to protect its residents from the thickening smoke. Luckily for them, even though the fire was now threatening the edge of the Bartolini property, the estate was vast.

When Vito had called her to let her know that the wildfire had spread and was now heading for the estate, she'd stopped job searching and immediately returned. She had no idea what she could do to help. She just knew she had to be here for Enzo.

After already having a close call with the baby, she wouldn't take any chances by going out to the front lines where they were doing everything possible to stave off the fire. But that didn't mean she couldn't cook for all the dislocated people seeking shelter at the estate or the men and women fighting to save it.

"Do you have more bread?" Anna, Vito's wife, asked. "The sandwiches are going fast."

"I have some that just came out of the oven," Sylvie said. "I don't know if it's cool enough."

Anna placed her hand on one of the loaves. "It's cool enough. These guys are hungry."

"I'll slice it up." Sylvie grabbed a knife and set to work thinly slicing the bread. She wished there was more she could do than just stand around working the kitchen. "Have they said how it's going? Are their efforts holding off the fire?"

"They said so far so good but that could change with a gust of wind."

The thought of it sent a shiver of apprehension skittering down her spine.

And then she realized that Enzo shouldn't be facing this nightmare alone. Sure, she was there, but she wasn't family. He needed his sisters.

She wasn't sure how Enzo would feel about her interfering, but lately she had the feeling he wasn't thinking clearly. He was being driven by ghosts of the past. Maybe it was time he was surrounded by the people who loved him here and now—his sisters…and her—even if he didn't love her in return.

She pulled her phone from her pocket. She had Bianca's number but not Gia's. She was certain once Bianca heard the news that she'd call her sister.

Sylvie hurriedly pressed Dial before she had a chance to talk herself out of it. The phone rang once, twice, three times. Her heart started to sink. Bianca was very busy these days, between planning her Christmas wedding and assuming her new royal duties.

But then the call was picked up and Bianca's voice came on the line. "Sylvie, hi. What's going on?"

"Bianca, thank goodness. Have you talked to your brother recently?"

"No, why?" Concern rang out in Bianca's voice. "What's wrong?"

"It's the estate. There's a wildfire…its headed for the villa."

Everything had changed.

And now it was about to change once more.

The speed at which Enzo's life was evolving was dizzying. He paused and leaned upon the shovel he'd been using to help widen the cleared property line between his estate and the neighbors', where the wildfire was wreaking utter devastation. He grabbed a rag from his back pocket to run across his sweaty brow.

He gazed out over the vineyard as a light layer of smoke mingled with the sun's rays. The sunlight bounced off the droplets of dew, making them sparkle as though the long lines of grapevines were in fact strung with glittering jewels.

It wasn't so long ago that this place had been his dream. He'd gone off to make a name for himself so that when he returned, his father would take him on as a full partner—respecting his input. But that day had never come. It was snatched away from both of them when a delivery truck ran a stop sign.

In the end Enzo had won the vineyard by default. It certainly didn't feel like a win. It definitely felt more like a tremendous loss—the loss of his parents, the loss of his idyllic vision of them, the loss of his love for these rolling hills and lush vines where he and his sisters used to go exploring.

A sound caught his attention. He glanced

over his shoulder. Caught up in his memories, for the briefest second he expected to see his sisters, Bianca and Gia, trekking their way toward him, laughing about something. When he'd ask what was so amusing, they'd shake their heads and say he wouldn't get it. But in reality, there was no one there. It was just a gust of hot, smoky wind rustling the leaves on the nearby vines.

Bianca had moved on. In just a few short months she would become the Princess of Patazonia. He hadn't been so sure about this love affair with a prince. In fact, he'd tried to keep them apart after Bianca returned from planning a royal wedding in Patazonia with a broken heart. But in the end, he saw that they truly belonged together.

And then there was his youngest sister, Gia. Her path to true love was not so simple. Not simple at all. To know that she'd been lied to all of her life by the people she was supposed to trust the most, their parents—it was unimaginable. And yet, through the darkest time in her life, she'd found love. Now both of his sisters were in committed relationships.

But not him—

"Enzo?"

He turned to find Vito standing there. He wasn't sure what to say to his manager, who was also the closest thing he had to a parent these days. He'd done what Vito had implored him not to do—sold the estate. Well, almost; pen had not been put to paper because of the wildfire.

Worry showed in Vito's eyes. "I wanted to let you know that the fire has really kicked up over the next hillside. They've thrown everything they've got at it. Perhaps it's time we pulled back."

"Did the firefighters tell us to move?" Enzo asked.

"Not yet. They said to be alert. They're trying to contain it before it gets this far."

"Good. Let's hope they succeed," Enzo said. "Tell our men, as always, it's totally their choice if they stay or go. I will understand if they need to go. But I'm staying until we're instructed otherwise." He paused and looked at his friend, dirt and sweat smeared on his aging face. "You should go, too."

Vito shook his head. "If you're staying, I am, too."

"I don't think that's a good idea." He pointed to the dark cloud in the distance. "You can see the fire isn't far off."

"I'm not leaving you out here alone."

"Have I told you lately how stubborn you are?" Then Enzo's gaze met Vito's. His voice softened. "Thank you for always being there."

"I'm not the only one who cares about you. I've seen the way Sylvie looks at you. It's the way my Anna looks at me."

He shook his head. "It's never going to work out." Not the romantic way. Even if the thought tempted him, he knew he'd ruined his chances with her. "She's gone."

"But it doesn't mean she can't come back. If you were to talk to her—tell her how you feel."

"Vito, now isn't the time."

His old friend nodded. "Just don't give up, on the estate or on Sylvie."

"I can't think about any of that now." Enzo turned back to the nightmare unfolding before him.

"I hope they're able to stop the fire before it reaches us."

"Me, too." Enzo didn't know why it should mean anything to him. After all, he was about to walk away from it. But he couldn't dismiss all the memories lurking all over the grounds. From birthday dinners that his mother had planned to his father teaching Enzo when he wasn't much more than a toddler about the soil and grapes.

For so long he hadn't wanted to relive those moments—the real moments that weren't tainted by lies. But Sylvie had slowly pulled back his blinders, seeing what had always been there in front of him. Family, happiness, anger, love and history. Theirs hadn't been a perfect family like he'd wanted to believe, but through it all, he'd felt loved.

"You know, for a man who doesn't care about the vineyard, you are fighting awfully hard to save it." And with that said, Vito walked off to check on the other men.

Enzo wanted to dismiss Vito's words, but as he got back to work, Vito's words haunted him. Why was he out here giving it his all? Why hadn't he paused for just two seconds to sign the sales agreement instead of springing out of the chair and rushing out the door as though the flames were licking at his heels?

How did Vito see through Enzo? It was like

the older man was telling him what he was afraid to admit to himself. In that moment Enzo finally acknowledged what his heart had known all along—he loved this estate with all its happy and sad memories because when they came together, it made for a life of loving and caring. And he loved Sylvie—even if he'd fought it for months because he was scared of letting himself become vulnerable once more and being hurt by someone else he cared about. And he loved the baby—even though he knew he was going to make mistakes along the way and not always have the answers.

Still, he wanted a second chance to make the estate a loving home for their baby—a second chance to show Sylvie just how much she meant to him. But was it too late for all of that?

CHAPTER SEVENTEEN

WHERE WAS ENZO?

Was he safe from the fire?

Sylvie sent up a prayer for his safety, as well as all the others out on the front lines. She'd just finished cleaning up after the midday food rush. In just a few minutes it'd be time to start preparing dinner.

She couldn't help but feel she wasn't doing enough. Her hand moved to her midsection; she had precious cargo on board that she had to make her priority. No one knew about the baby yet but Enzo. It wasn't that she didn't want to tell people—she did. She was so excited about the baby, but there was a part of her waiting until she'd worked out things with Enzo before she spread the joyous news.

As she stood on the veranda, her favorite spot in the villa, she noticed the smoke in the distance was practically gone. She squinted. Was that right? Was the fire diminishing?

Hope swelled in her chest. For the past three days that was what she and everyone else at the Bartolini estate had been praying for. Had their prayers finally been answered?

But they weren't the only ones praying. Bianca and Gia were, too. Both sisters had dropped everything and flown in immediately following Sylvie's call. All three of them, along with Vito's wife, had been working side by side in the kitchen, making sure everyone was fed and as comfortable as was possible under the circumstances.

"Did you hear the news?" Bianca rushed out onto the veranda, all smiles.

"News?" Sylvie hadn't heard anything. As soon as the kitchen was squared away, she'd slipped out here for a little quiet time.

"The best news." Gia stepped up beside her sister.

They may only be half-sisters according to biology, but their facial features were similar, from the set of their eyes to their pert noses and full lips. And their relationship was so close that they could finish each other's sentences.

The news of Gia's conception had undoubtedly been devastating, but it appeared the sisters had recovered and were closer than ever. Now, if only Enzo would come around, maybe he wouldn't be in such a rush to put all of this behind him.

Anxious to know the news, Sylvie said, "Well, don't just smile at me, tell me what's happening. Is it the fire? Is it out?"

"Not out," Bianca said, the smile slipping from her face.

"But contained," Gia added.

"And the vineyard, was it spared?"

The sisters' expressions creased with worry lines.

"We haven't heard from any of the men," Bianca said. "But they should be back soon."

"And the evacuation order has been lifted so everyone is packing to head back home," Gia said. "Except for us. We've talked it over and we're sticking around for a while."

"I'm sure Enzo will appreciate it." Sylvie's thoughts turned to Enzo, wondering if she should leave before he returned. "I know he's missed both of you."

Bianca glanced down at her clasped hands. "Yeah, we really messed up forgetting his birthday."

"It won't happen again," Gia said emphatically. "We added it to our calendars on our phones."

"No matter where we are, we'll always remember," Bianca said.

Sylvie nodded in understanding. "Well, now that everything is under control and you two are sticking around, I should go pack."

"You're leaving?" both sisters asked in unison.

Sylvie lowered her gaze and nodded. "I need to get back to Florence."

"Stay," the sisters said at once.

To be a part of this family would be like a dream come true, and it had nothing to do with their vast wealth or Bianca's becoming a real-life princess or Gia's living on a romantic island in the Mediterranean or the way Enzo cared for his sisters like some mother hen. No, it had everything to do with the love that abounded among the three siblings, keeping them together through their parents' deaths, through a strange codicil to their will and through the discovery of an earthshattering secret. To be a part of a love that strong is something most people could only dream of.

Gia moved to Sylvie's side and put her arm around her. "What's wrong?"

"What?" Sylvie had been so deep in her thoughts that she hadn't realized her distress had shown on her face.

"You're crying." Bianca's eyes displayed concern.

Sylvie pressed her fingertips to her cheeks, feeling the dampness. She swiped away the tears. These pregnancy hormones had her crying at the drop of a hat. "It's nothing."

"Enzo might believe that line, but we don't." Bianca crossed her arms as though letting her know she meant business. "Talk to us. Is it our brother? Has he upset you?"

Maybe she should tell them. After all, they were the baby's aunts. The urge to confess swelled within her until it was a loud roar in her ears.

"I'm pregnant with Enzo's baby." The words just came tumbling out.

Both women's mouths opened and for a moment no words came. They looked at each other. And then their attention returned to Sylvie.

After a moment Bianca pressed her lips

together as though she was gathering her thoughts. "Does Enzo know?"

Sylvie nodded. "It was a shock for both of us."

"And what did he say?"

"Not a lot at first. Then he said he was calling off the sale of the estate. I told him not to. The baby wasn't reason enough to change his mind—to remain someplace he doesn't want to be. I don't want him blaming me or the baby for his having to stay here."

"He wouldn't do that," Bianca said.

"I never believed that he wanted to leave here," Gia said. "When we were kids all he talked about was one day running the vineyard just like Papá."

"Do you love our brother?" Bianca asked.

Without hesitation, Sylvie said, "Yes."

They talked for a little more about the baby and Enzo. Both Bianca and Gia encouraged her to give Enzo some more time. They were certain once he got over the shock that things would look different for both of them.

"I can't stay here and hope he'll fall in love with me." Sylvie took a step toward the doorway. “I have to go make a life for the baby and myself.”

Concern filled Bianca’s gaze. “Isn’t there anything we can say to get you to stay? I’m sure Enzo will want to see you and thank you for all you did.”

Sylvie shook her head. “It’s best I go.”

And with that, she walked away, feeling as though she were leaving a part of her behind—her heart. But Enzo had made his decision. When Vito had called to let her know the wildfire was threatening the estate, he’d told her that Enzo was meeting with the buyer to sign the sales agreement. Nothing had changed Enzo’s mind about staying here—not her and not the baby.

CHAPTER EIGHTEEN

LEAVING THIS TIME was harder than the first time.

Sylvie packed her few things in her bag. She couldn't help feeling things with Enzo were going to get more complicated before they figured out a way to peacefully co-parent. She didn't even know what that would be like if he were to move to France, but for their child's sake, they'd figure it out.

It was then that she realized she was folding and refolding the same shirt because there was a part of her that was hoping to see Enzo before she left. Though another part insisted it would be easier on everyone if she quietly slipped away. His sisters would be here for him. With that thought in mind, she hurriedly placed the rest of her clothes in the bag and zipped it.

Knock-knock.

Sylvie figured it was Bianca or Gia, who were once more going to try and convince her to stay. “Come in.” At that point she realized she’d forgot her sunglasses on top of the chest of drawers. She turned to retrieve them, confident that at last she had gathered all of her things. She turned back around, surprised to find Enzo standing just inside the doorway. “Enzo, you’re back.”

He nodded. It was then she noticed the dark streaks of soot on his face, his scattered hair and his disheveled clothes. “My sisters told me you were getting ready to leave. Weren’t you even going to stick around and say hello before you left?”

Her gaze searched his. What was he trying to say? Was he disappointed she was trying to avoid him? Or was that just wishful thinking on her part?

“I… I didn’t want to get in the way.” She glanced down at her bag, opening the side pocket to place her sunglasses inside. “I’m sure you have a lot of catching up to do with your sisters.”

“Do you even want to know how the estate faired?”

Immediately, her gaze rose to meet his. “Of course. Were you able to save it all?”

He shook his head. There was a torrent of emotions in his eyes but she wasn't able to distinguish one from the other. He reached up and rubbed the back of his neck. "We lost some vines."

"I'm sorry." She truly was sorry. "Hopefully, they can be replanted."

He nodded. "It'll take time but it's doable."

"I'm sure the new owner will be relieved." She lifted her bag and swung the strap over her shoulder. It was time to make a quick exit while she still had her emotions in check.

"Sylvie, there isn't going to be a new owner."

"There isn't? But I thought the papers had been signed."

"I got called away before we signed the papers. You might say the whole deal went up in flames." A half smile pulled at his lips.

Her heart was pounding. What did this mean? She refused to jump to conclusions. She wasn't going to get her hopes up just to have them dashed. After all, there was a baby counting on her to get this right.

"You could stay on, here at the estate," he said.

She shook her head. "I need to return to Florence and continue searching for a new job."

"And the baby?"

"I would never keep you away from him or her. Florence isn't that far away. I'm sure we can work out a visitation schedule."

"You won't reconsider staying here?"

She gave a firm shake of her head. "I have to start a new life for myself and the baby. It's better this way."

If she were to stay here, she didn't think she'd ever be able to get over Enzo. He'd always be around. They'd be bumping into each other at every turn. And a one-way love—it just wasn't enough for her.

Even though her parents' love had burned bright and quickly, it was something genuine—something so strong that her mother held on to the memories of that love until her last breath. If Sylvie was going to risk her heart to another, she wanted a strong, passionate love like theirs had been.

"I… I understand." Though the tone of his voice seemed to say the opposite. "I'll take care of the rent—"

"No, Enzo. I told you I'll take care of myself."

"But that's my baby you're carrying."

"It's mine, too, and I'll make sure we're taken care of."

He turned to her and frowned. "Why are you being so stubborn?"

Her mouth gaped. It took her a moment to gather herself, but that didn't stop her from glaring at him. "I'm not."

"All I'm trying to do is my part as far as the baby is concerned, but you won't let me. If you think I'm not going to support my own child and not be there as much as possible, you're very wrong."

"I would never stop you from being there for our child. I… I just need to do this transition on my own." She needed to prove to herself that she could do this because being a single mother scared her. She remembered how hard her mother had worked to provide for her, and she worried that she wouldn't be able to give her son or daughter as good a life as her mother had given her.

"But that's the thing. You don't have to do it

alone—you don't have to do any of this alone. Marry me."

What had he said?

Her gaze searched his to see if it was some sort of joke. But the look on Enzo's face said he was perfectly serious. He wanted to marry her.

She needed to hear that he loved her as much as she loved him. She wouldn't accept anything less. Then she would make a home with him—have a family with him.

"Why?" she asked.

"Why what? Why get married?" When she nodded, he visibly swallowed. He wasn't comfortable with this conversation. That was her first warning. He cleared his throat. "We're having a baby. Isn't that reason enough?"

No, it wasn't reason enough. Not even close to it. There was so much more to a marriage than children. And if their union wasn't founded in love, how were they ever to make it through the storms life threw their way? Their marriage would get blown off course and flounder.

He approached her. His gaze beseeched hers. "Sylvie, marry me."

With strength she didn't know she possessed, she said, "No."

Before her pregnancy hormones realized what she'd just done and sent her into a fit of tears, she stepped around him. With her head held high, she headed for the door. Inside, her facade was starting to melt. It was a good thing she'd already arranged for a ride into the city because if she stayed here any longer, she might change her mind. And that wouldn't be good for any of them—including the baby.

Goodbye.

She didn't say the word. She didn't trust her voice as there was a giant lump in her throat. Instead, she blinked back the tears and kept walking.

CHAPTER NINETEEN

No.

One single syllable. Two tiny letters.

Combined, they had the power to deeply pierce his scarred heart.

Enzo stumbled as he made his way to the kitchen. He walked blindly as all his resources were focused on reviewing exactly what had gone wrong with their conversation. It shouldn't have gone so far off the tracks. He'd gone over it word for word while out in the fields. He'd been certain Sylvie would see that marrying him was the best option. She loved the estate and had been happy here. At least, that was what he'd thought. If she would have agreed to marry him, they'd have lived happily ever after right here in this very house.

But when he'd rushed back to the villa to share news that the fire had been defeated, all those well-planned, well-chosen words had gone straight out of his head. At first, he'd been caught up in the beautiful sight of her. It was in that moment he realized just how much he'd missed her. He'd missed talking to her, listening to the lilt of her voice and her laughter, it was contagious.

But today had been different. She'd been different. He'd noticed the stubborn jut of her chin and the pain in her eyes. He should have realized it wasn't going to be so easy to rectify the past. But he'd been so wound up, so ready to profess his well-planned words.

Yet, when he opened his mouth those words he'd planned…well, they'd gotten all jumbled up somewhere between his brain and his tongue. And maybe he had rushed things a bit with that proposal. But she was being stubborn and he'd grown more nervous with each passing moment.

He knew she loved the estate—enough to wage a campaign to stop him from selling it. So the only reason he could come up with for her to turn him down was that she didn't love him. Maybe she cared about him as a friend, but she couldn't see him as anything more than that—

"Enzo, what's wrong?"

He didn't have to lift his head to recognize that voice. It was Bianca. When his gaze rose, he found not one but both sisters staring at him with worry reflected in their eyes.

"Where's Sylvie?" Gia asked.

"She left." His voice sounded hollow as he slumped down in a kitchen chair.

"Left?" Bianca said. "I thought you were going to talk to her."

He lowered his gaze to the tabletop. "I did."

"And she still left?" Gia pulled out a chair across the table from him.

"She did."

Bianca sat next to him. "Why didn't you stop her?"

His gaze jerked up to meet hers. Frustration bunched up in his gut. "Don't you think I tried? I even told her we should get married."

Bianca and Gia turned to each other. They didn't say a word, but they were communicating nonetheless. He hated when they did this and left him out. He had no idea what they were thinking—no, that wasn't true. He knew what they thought. He screwed this all up. And he couldn't disagree.

His chair scraped over the slate floor tiles.

"Don't go." Bianca stood, as if to follow him.

He shook his head. "I don't need you to tell me that I've made a mess of everything—starting when we were kids."

"When we were kids?" Bianca sent him a puzzled look.

"What are you talking about?" Gia moved to Bianca's side.

He hadn't meant to bring up the past. He'd just been so worked up and the words had come tumbling out. It was a mistake. But how was he going to take it back now that his sisters were laser focused on him?

And then he heard the echo of Sylvie's voice urging him to open up about the past. She'd told him to be honest with his sisters about everything and trust that they'd make it through another revelation.

But the thought of revealing the secret he'd been keeping more than half his life was daunting. His gut knotted up. What if they never spoke to him again?

"Enzo, talk to us." Bianca's voice drew him from his internal debate.

"You better sit down for this," he said in a resigned tone.

His sisters exchanged worried glances as they took a seat. And then he told them about that long-ago night when he'd overheard his parents' argument about their mother's affair. It was a memory he hoped he'd never have to revisit after today.

Silence greeted his confession. And it stretched out into an uncomfortable void.

Enzo shifted in his seat. "I'm really sorry. I've messed up big-time."

Bianca's fine brows drew together. "You really thought they were talking about you?"

He nodded.

"Is this why you've been acting so strange?" Gia asked. "Why you look like you've been carrying around the weight of the world?"

He shrugged and then nodded. "I'd put that memory out of my mind. I'd convinced myself it was just a horrible dream. And when you want to believe something enough, it's pretty easy to do." He paused and drew in a deep breath. He had one more admission to make. "And then when the journal was found, the memory came back. I… I should have said something then. But I was…afraid."

Another awkward silence filled the air. What

were they thinking? Would they understand? Or would they remain angry with him?

Knock-knock.

Enzo inwardly groaned. Now wasn't the time for interruptions. He needed to work this out with his sisters—sisters who were being unusually quiet. It wasn't a good sign.

Bianca jumped up. "I think it's Mr. Caruso."

"What's the family attorney doing here?" Enzo asked. And then a thought came to him. "Does this have to do with the sale of the estate?"

"I don't know," Bianca said. "He called earlier and asked if he could drop by."

"Do you think it's something bad?" Gia asked as they all moved toward the front door.

No one answered her question. Enzo hoped Gia was wrong. They'd already had enough bad stuff to last a lifetime.

Bianca swung the door open and greeted Mr. Caruso. His face was pale and drawn as though he had a matter of great importance weighing on his mind.

After they ushered him into Enzo's office because the living room was still a bit disheveled from their guests, Enzo turned to the older man. "What's wrong?"

"I don't know quite how this happened." Mr. Caruso started to pace. "It really shouldn't have happened. In all my years as an attorney, I've never seen something like this." The man's words were rushed.

"Sit down." Gia guided him over to a chair. As she stood behind the chair as the man took a seat, she raised her brows at her siblings. She then moved to a nearby chair to sit down.

Mr. Caruso clutched his leather satchel with both arms. "I'm so sorry. I had to replace my assistant a while back and it took a few candidates until I found one that was a good fit. I don't know if it happened then or what—"

"It's okay." Enzo sat behind what had been their father's desk. "Just tell us the problem and we'll go from there."

Mr. Caruso searched through his satchel and pulled out a legal-size envelope. He held it up. "This was supposed to have been with your parents' will. Somehow it got misplaced."

"What is it?" Enzo hesitantly asked, wondering if it was yet another bombshell.

Gia frowned. "We're not sure we want to learn any more family secrets."

"I agree," Bianca chimed in. "It's been a roller-coaster year. Maybe you should just keep whatever that is."

Mr. Caruso looked perplexed. "I… I can't do that." He stood and held out the envelope to no one in particular. "Who should I give it to?"

Neither Enzo nor his sisters reached for it.

Mr. Caruso placed the envelope on the edge of the desk. "I'll just leave it here until one of you feels like reading it. Again, I'm so sorry about this."

Not one of the three of them spoke. They sat there staring at the envelope as though at any moment it was going to explode. Dread consumed Enzo. Hadn't they already been through enough?

"I'll see myself out." Mr. Caruso made a hasty departure.

Enzo wasn't sure how long they just sat there staring at the envelope wondering what bit of dynamite it contained. Would reading it once again blow apart their worlds?

Gia sat forward. "This is ridiculous. We can't pretend we don't know it exists. And we can't spend the next year or so wondering what it says."

Enzo cleared his throat. "I agree." He turned his attention to Bianca. "If we're going to do this, it needs to be unanimous. What do you say?"

Bianca hesitated before she nodded in agreement. Gia did the same.

Enzo reached for the envelope. Across the front, each of their names were printed in their father's handwriting. Enzo's gut twisted into a knot.

Here we go again.

He stuck his finger beneath the flap and yanked, opening the envelope. His heart pounded in his chest as he recalled the nightmare that had unfolded after they read their mother's journal.

Please don't let this be like that.

Enzo withdrew two sheets of paper with his father's handwriting. His instinct was to skim through the letter and make sure there was nothing that was going to upset his sisters, but he knew that wasn't fair to them. Hadn't he already learned the price of keeping secrets?

Enzo cleared his throat and began reading aloud.

"Enzo, Bianca and Gia, I apologize for what you have gone through with the contest to win the estate. Your mother told me not to do it, but I didn't want any of you to make a life-altering mistake like your mother and I have done. By fighting for the villa you've each had a chance to figure out what the place means to you. I know that each of you loves the estate, perhaps for different reasons, and that's okay. But without the contest it would be easy for each of you to forget its meaning. Just as your mother and I became so complacent in our marriage that for a moment we forgot what it meant to both of us. I can tell you all that your mother is the love of my life. And I believe she feels the same for me. We experienced troubles in our time. I would say it was my fault, though she would vehemently disagree. I had become so absorbed in growing the vineyard that I forgot about the importance of family. My fatherly advice to each of you is not to for-

get your family is your priority. Their love, safety and happiness must come first. Always. If you're reading this letter, it means your mother and I are no longer with you. But never doubt we're looking down upon each of you, cheering you on and loving you all. And hoping that each of you finds the one great love in your life like your mother and I have done. I hope by now the three of you have found your way back to being family once more. That was our final parting gift—by pulling you apart, the three of you would come back together closer than ever. We love you. We always will.
Papá and Mamma."

When Enzo finished reading the letter, stunned silence filled the room. His sisters swiped at their damp eyes. Enzo blinked repeatedly.

It took Enzo time to absorb what he'd read. His parents may have made mistakes but how could he hold that against them when he'd been making one mistake after the next?

And then he remembered something else his

father had told him: *Family means not giving up. No matter what.*

"I may not agree with Papá's methods," Bianca said, breaking the silence, "but he's right. I feel closer to both of you than I have since we were kids."

"I agree," Gia said.

Enzo wasn't sure he'd heard them correctly. "You mean you aren't mad at me for not speaking up about the secret?"

His breath caught in his chest as he waited for their collective answer. He knew he didn't deserve a pass. If it had been reversed and they'd kept him in the dark, he'd have been very upset. But it didn't keep him from hoping for forgiveness.

"You should have told us," Gia said.

"You should have trusted us." Bianca looked more hurt than angry.

"But it's over now. And you have to let this go," Gia said, "before you're so busy looking over your shoulder at the past that you miss your future."

"She's right," Bianca said. "Sylvie told us everything."

His eyes widened. "Sylvie told you about the baby?"

Bianca nodded. "She did. She said she was going to sit on the news until you two figured things out, but she just couldn't hold it in any longer."

"Sylvie should be here with you—with us." Gia's pointed stare was directed right at him. "If you don't go get her, I will."

"But the estate—"

"Will be fine while you're gone," Bianca jumped in. "We'll take care of things here."

"And if you want," Gia said, "I can start renovations to turn this place back into the home we once knew it to be."

The thought appealed to him. Maybe that was why he'd felt such a disconnect with the estate—his home no longer felt like a home but rather the hotel it'd become. "You would do that?"

Gia smiled and nodded. "I'd love to."

Love for his sisters lifted the corners of his mouth. "I don't know how to thank you."

Gia's gaze met his. "Easy. Go get your family."

Enzo made his way to his room to shower

and pack. He was off to the city. But how was he supposed to prove to Sylvie that he'd always be there for her and the baby?

Then he realized he couldn't just expect Sylvie to change her plans once more; he knew he was the one who would have to make the concession this time. And a plan started to take shape.

CHAPTER TWENTY

SHE MISSED HIS smile and the warmth of his deep laugh.

She missed the estate with its picturesque rolling hills and the horses.

She missed all of it.

Sylvie stuffed the sad thoughts to the back of her mind. That was her past. This was her future. It had been a week since she'd turned down Enzo's marriage proposal.

But was it a proposal? Not really. Traditionally, it would involve popping the question and he hadn't asked her anything. Enzo's mention of marriage was more akin to suggesting a restaurant for dinner.

A marriage proposal should be filled with emotion. Love should be mentioned—in fact, it should take center stage. It didn't have to be delivered on bended knee. A ring would be nice but not a requirement. However, for her the love part was nonnegotiable.

Knock-knock.

Sylvie turned from where she was washing her lunch dishes. She didn't have to answer the door to know who was on the other side of it. The delivery guy from the florist downstairs.

Every day that week, Enzo had sent her flowers with little messages.

The first had said *I'm sorry.*

The next had said *I want to make things up to you.*

Each new bouquet came with a note:

I'm working on a surprise.
Please give me another chance.
It won't be much longer.

And finally…

I miss you.

She had to admit it was like getting pieces of a love letter. She grew anxious to know what today's message would be. She realized that a true love letter should say he loved her and so far that hadn't been the case.

She moved to the door and opened it. There stood Vincenzo, who worked downstairs in the flower shop. He was the owner's grandson, who was planning to one day take over the family business.

He smiled. "These are for you."

She accepted the red rosebuds. She paused to sniff them. They made her smile. Red roses meant love. Was Enzo working up to tell her he loved her?

She turned and paused, trying to figure out where to put them. "You do know I'm starting to run out of room."

"I think the guy has it really bad for you. Maybe you should give him another chance."

She had to admit the flowers were wearing down her resolve, but she had to wonder when Enzo was going to make his plea in person. "I just might do that."

She was anxious for Vincenzo to go. She wanted to read the attached card in private, even though Vincenzo was the one who had written it and attached it to the bouquet.

Vincenzo hesitated as though he wanted to say more, then he wished her a good day and moved on.

Sylvie closed the door before rushing over to the small kitchen table. She placed the vase on the counter and then reached for the envelope. With each bouquet and note, she felt her excitement rise. What would he say today?

She opened the little envelope and pulled out the card.

The surprise is ready. Below is the address and time. Please come.

Frustration balled up in her stomach. She didn't want to wait. What exactly did he have planned? With Enzo it could be anything. But she'd never been so excited for anything in her life.

She placed her hand over her tiny baby bump. "We're going to see your daddy today, little one. I don't know how it'll work out, but I promise, no matter what, we're both going to love you with all of our hearts."

He wasn't sure this was going to work.

He wasn't even sure she would show up.

Enzo straightened his tie for the fourth or fifth time. Maybe he should have invited her to dinner in person. But he'd hoped to capture her attention with the notes. But did it work? Would she show up?

He'd been working nonstop on this surprise since he'd arrive in Florence a week ago. Gia had phoned a few times to ask his input on the renovations at the villa. They were growing closer once more. It sounded like she already had a line on some workers to launch the project. With the villa safely in his sister's hands, he could focus on his own work.

He'd paid double-time to have a crew work round the clock on his surprise for Sylvie. It wasn't complete, but it was far enough along that she would get the idea.

He moved to the table in the middle of the room with the white tablecloth and two red taper candles. He'd already lit them. Maybe that was a mistake. What if she was late? The candles would melt down and not look nice. But he'd wanted to have the mood set for when she arrived—if she arrived.

"Mr. Bartolini—" the head of a string quartet approached him with a violin in hand "—would you like us to begin playing?"

"Not yet. You can start just as soon as—" What did he call her? His girlfriend? The mother of his baby? "—as soon as my guest arrives."

If she shows up…

He had caterers in the back keeping food warm to serve an elegant, hopefully long dinner. He'd tried to pull out all of the stops tonight, but to be honest, he'd never planned an evening like this so he wasn't sure if he was missing anything or not.

He started to pace. He yanked at his buttoned collar. It felt too tight. He wasn't sure about any of this, including his suit. Maybe he should—

Tinkle. Tinkle.

The bell above the front door alerted him that someone had arrived.

Please let it be Sylvie.

He turned and in the dimmed light, he made out her very familiar petite form. Boy, had he missed her. He'd missed everything about her. But tonight wasn't about him; it was about her. And showing her that he was the right man for her.

She'd checked the address three times.

It was a storefront. And it didn't look occupied. Though the soft glow of light shone through the white curtains over the windows.

Certain she had the right place, Sylvie opened

the door. A little bell rang out her arrival. She stepped inside. The overhead lights were dimmed and a violin started playing. What in the world…?

Her gaze moved to the single table in the middle of the room. There were two table settings and candles. In the center of the table was a bud vase with a single long-stem red rose. Her heart swooned. Had Enzo set all of this up for her? And where was he?

It was then that he stepped out of the shadows and approached her. He smiled but it didn't quite reach his eyes. Was he as nervous as she was?

"Thank you for coming," he said.

"Enzo, what is all of this?"

"This is my new store, Barto Wines."

"You're opening a wine store?"

He nodded. "It's something that I'd been planning to mention to my father when he had his accident. I abandoned the idea while trying to navigate the aftermath of my parents' deaths. But now seemed to be the right time to move to Florence—"

"You're moving here?" That was something

she hadn't expected. Not at all. "But why not France, like you'd talked about?"

He peered deep into her eyes, making her heart beat faster. "I have an apartment upstairs. No matter what you or the baby need, I will be here. Day or night."

"But…but you can't do that. What about your life? Your dreams?"

"That's what I'm trying to tell you. My dreams revolve around you." He stepped closer. "I'm sorry for how I handled things. It took my sisters and my parents to point out the mistakes I've been making. I've talked to my sisters about the past, like you suggested."

Hope swelled in her chest. "How did it go?"

"It wasn't easy, but just like you predicted, they forgave me."

"I'm so happy to hear that."

"And now it's time I apologize to you, for being such a fool." He stared deep into her eyes, making her heart pound. "I've made one mistake after the next and I probably don't deserve a second chance, but I've learned my lesson and I promise I'm going to be honest with you and support you, no matter what. And I'll always be there for our little one."

He was saying all the right words. Perhaps she should say something, too, but she didn't want to interrupt him, not when she had the feeling he was about to tell her something very important.

"Sylvie, I love you." Her heart swooned as he continued. "I think I've loved you since you arrived in Tuscany. How could I not with your glowing smile and infectious laugh? You light up my days like no one else has ever done. And without you in my life, it's all shades of gray."

She stared into his eyes, making sure she hadn't just imagined the words he'd spoken. But his eyes showed his love. "I love you, too."

He let out a visible breath. "I was hoping you'd say that. You don't know how worried I was that I'd screwed up everything."

"You didn't screw anything up. Things are working out just like I always imagined they would."

He leaned toward her just as she lifted up on her tiptoes and pressed her lips to his. Tears of joy dampened her eyes. Right now she was a trembling ball of excitement. Her dream was coming true. And then much too soon, Enzo pulled back.

"Hold that thought. I have one more surprise." He pulled a small remote from his pocket. With the press of a button, a dazzling array white lights in a star pattern moved across the ceiling and walls. He held out a hand to her. "Would you dance with me?"

She nodded, afraid words would fail her. She placed her hand in his and he pulled her close. Her heart was pounding so hard in her ears that she couldn't hear the music. She followed Enzo's lead as they made their way around the floor.

This was what her mother had always meant about finding that one great love in your life. Sylvie never could have guessed it would feel this good. She was head over heels in love.

When the music stopped, Enzo dropped to one knee just like in a movie. "Sylvie, I haven't always said the right thing or done the right thing, but I hope you'll be able to see past my mistakes and know that I love you with all of my heart." He reached in his jacket pocket and held a diamond ring out to her. "Will you do me the greatest honor of being my partner in life?"

Tears of joy clouded her eyes. She blinked

because she didn't want to miss any of this. "Yes. Yes, I'll marry you."

He slipped the ring on her trembling finger and then he straightened. He smiled at her as she swiped away her happy tears. "How did I get to be so lucky?"

"I'm the lucky one to have you in my life."

"But where will we live? Your apartment? Or mine?"

He smiled. "Wherever you want, but I do know of this villa and vineyard that would be perfect for a growing family."

"Really?" She felt so very blessed in that moment and hoped her mother was looking down over her, seeing her get her happily-ever-after.

He nodded. And then he leaned forward, pressing his lips to hers.

EPILOGUE

Kingdom of Patazonia, December 20

THIS WAS IT.

The big day had arrived.

Bianca Bartolini's stomach shivered with nerves. She stood in the preparation room in the Grand Cathedral of Patazonia surrounded by the family she'd been born into and those she chose to call family. And as much as she wished her parents were here, she knew they were watching down over her. Of that, she was certain.

She'd stood in this very room before. It had been in her position as a wedding planner. She'd been nervous back then, too, but for a totally different reason.

Today she was the bride. *The bride.* A big smile pulled at her lips. The thought of being Leo's wife excited her beyond belief. It was the responsibilities that went with the position that made her nervous, though she tried to hide it from everyone. Her self-doubts were still there, lurking in the background. She was about to become a princess. The thought stole her breath away.

Most of all, she was grateful that her rapidly expanding family was with her. She smiled as her gaze moved around the room. She'd be lost without their unfailing love and support.

"Love looks good on you." Gia smiled.

"I'm truly happy." Bianca's gaze landed on her younger sister, who was glowing with happiness. "And I have a feeling it won't be long until we're at your wedding."

Gia's face filled with color as she glanced away.

"Gia, what aren't you telling me? Are you already engaged?"

The color in her face deepened. "Not exactly."

"What's that supposed to mean?"

Gia hesitated as though she was trying to figure out how to answer her. Just as Bianca was about to prompt her sister, Gia said, "We've talked about getting married."

"And?"

"That's as far as it got. I've been busy working on remodeling houses and he's been busy with his new algorithm."

Bianca reached out and squeezed her sister's hand. "He's good for you. I see how you light up around him. Don't put off the important things in life." Her thoughts strayed to her parents and how life could be so unexpected.

The smile fell from Gia's face. "You aren't the only one thinking of Mamma and Papá today." She swiped at her eyes. "But I think they're here. I can see Papá when Enzo smiles. And I see Mamma in your eyes."

"And I see both of them in you. The patience you have is so like Papá. And your talent for making everything look perfect is just like Mamma."

"What have we missed?" Enzo stepped up to them with his new bride.

Enzo and Sylvie had had a small ceremony at the villa as soon as Gia had completed the renovations. Instead of being here at Bianca's wedding, they should be off on their much-deserved honeymoon. But they'd delayed their departure until after the New Year. They both agreed that there was nowhere else in the world they'd want to be right now.

Sylvie had officially given up her wedding planner business. With Enzo's encouragement she was following her dreams and designing wedding dresses full-time. In fact, Bianca was wearing a Sylvie Original.

Bianca made sure to tell everyone that Sylvie was a rising star. Orders were already pouring in after seeing a few of Sylvie's designs. Just wait until the world saw Bianca's royal wedding gown.

"You just missed our little sister getting worked up," Bianca lightly teased her brother.

"I was not," Gia said as if by instinct. "Okay. Maybe a little. It's just that our little family is growing. And Mamma and Papá aren't here to see it."

"They're here," Enzo said. "They're definitely here."

With that, the door opened and the royal wedding planner stepped into the room. "Everyone out. Except you—" she pointed to Bianca "—and you." She pointed to Enzo, who was to walk her down the aisle. "The ceremony is about to begin."

Bianca hugged Gia and then she hugged Sylvie.

"Oh!" Sylvie paused.

"Is something wrong?" Enzo was by her side instantly.

Sylvie smiled. "Nothing is wrong. Everything is right. That was just our little football player in there, letting me know he's awake."

"It's a boy?" Bianca and Gia asked simultaneously.

"Oops." She glanced at her husband. "I thought you told them."

He shook his head. "I didn't get a chance with all of the wedding stuff."

Bianca rushed forward. First, she hugged her brother and then Sylvie. "Congratulations. I have a feeling this coming year is going to be absolutely amazing."

"I agree," Gia said.

The room cleared as the procession music began to play. This past year had been full of highs and lows but through it all, she and her siblings had stuck together. Bianca's heart was full of love. It was only going to get better from here.

And now it was time for her to go marry her

very own Prince Charming. She placed her hand on the crook of her brother's arm. She couldn't help but think of her father when she looked at Enzo. They were so similar in looks and mannerisms. Her heart swelled with love.

The two large wooden doors swung open and Bianca stepped into her future. When her gaze connected with Leo's, her heart fluttered in her chest. Her insecurities faded away. All she felt now was love. Love for her new country, love for her family and most of all love for the prince of her heart.

* * * * *